The Adventures of Toshin & Dhyum

The Sorceress of Sarpatta

Omi

ISBN
Paperback 979-8-89961-619-8
Hardcase 979-8-89961-620-4

Dedication

To the beautiful Kusum in my life, may you find your

'Everlasting Happiness'

Contents

Contents

1. Almagri

1

Almagri

There were noises that night, oh yes the night sky was filled with the distant howling of the coyotes that had decided to come out in force and show their presence. Not to be outdone, their howls were answered by the strays of Almagri.

The man moving stealthily in the shadows recognized the lone howl of a wolf amoung the chorus of howls. He remembered the wolf well but he had no time to reminisce now. He had a task at hand and he had to see it through.

His treaded softly through the cobbled moonlit street. He kept to the shadows and his dark eyes scanned the horizon and his immediate vicinity by virtue of habit. He avoided the wider well-lit and well manned main streets to the alley ways of the old bazaar. The bazaar was now closed and the only sounds that came from the closed tarpaulins were the snores of the bazar coolies and the sleepy rambling of a few drunks.

His face was covered with his dark turban cloth that not only to give him anonymity but it also stopped him from inhaling the strong aroma of the various spices that were stored in the now closed bazaar. He could not risk a sneeze lest he wake up one of the sleeping workers.

He slowed down as he approached the main street and waited in the shadow motionless, his body pressed to the wall of a vegetable and flower warehouse. The rough texture of the wall pricked his back and the foul stink from the vegetable waste dumped nearby hit his senses hard. But he had learned to ignore these inconveniences like the large rodent that had climbed his feet unknowingly and scurried away the moment he had wriggled his toe to let it know that he was not a stone mural.

His ability to remain motionless in these situations had saved him from many a tricky and some dangerous situations. He looked up at the crescent moon and estimated the time to be close to 2am. The right time for 'Bhutas' and 'Pretas' *(Spirit beings)* to venture out he smiled to himself as he slowly undid the rest of his turban letting his long wavy hair settle on his shoulders. He then adjusted the unfurled turban around his face leaving only his sharp dark eyes visible. He often used the cover of the dark with the hope of being mistaken for a Bhuta if ever some unsuspecting soul had seen him moving silently in the shadows.

He moved swiftly again as soon as he was satisfied that he was alone and rounded the main street towards an imposing building with an equally imposing boundary wall made of square cut stones. There were armed guards at the huge cast iron gate which was easily two heads tall and spiked. He slowed down and watched the huge window on the first floor which had an open balcony. The curtain was drawn and no light came out of them, satisfied he walked stealthily around the compound wall and stopped by a spot. A mango tree branch was jutting out from the boundary wall and onto the pavement. He looked around quickly and removed a pair of metal spikes from the belt around his waist. His belt carried an assortment of hooks and other bits. He wore dark clothes in which he could move freely and yet they were not too loose to impair his movements. He had let his shoulder length hair untied and open to add to the illusion of a Preta. He had never come across a Bhuta or Preta himself but he imagined the Preta's would not be adorning their heads with a turban if ever there was one.

'This obsession with turbans in Almagri is really getting out of hand' he scoffed inwardly. Though it was a proud tradition of Almagri to wear the royal emblem of the Leaping Stallion on the turban during special occasions it had slowly converged into a show of upmanship and opulence by wearing the most elaborate and in his mind ridiculously cumbersome head gears.

The turban was now a tool to announce your standing in society and some considered it a personal insult if the person they were meeting decided to meet them in a simple turban or god forbid bare headed. The well healed merchants and royal officials made it a point to wear silk turbans with the Royal emblem 'The Leaping Stallion' sticking out in an elaborate golden pin with precious stones. They would adorn it with pearls, rubies and garnets.

The less fastidious folks wore caps and turbans that suited the weather and their profession but all covered their crown when they stepped out of their houses in Almagri.

He now tied his open hair into a tight knot and quickly attached the two metal spikes to the front of each of his shoes.

At first sight his feet looked bare but on close inspection it looked like he had grown an extra layer of skin, but in reality he had wrapped a tough skin like material tightly around his feet which reached upto his ankles.

He had designed and made his footwear himself to fit the contours of his feet perfectly. It gave him the flexibility to scramble, climb, run and even swim if required with his footwear.

While attaching the spikes to his feet he kept his ears open to listen to the movement of the guard who would be reaching his spot anytime now, and right on cue he heard the approaching footsteps of the guard. He quickly placed his spiked feet on a crack in between the stones and quickly climbed up the wall expertly in impressive time. He perched easily and quietly on the branch of the mango tree and watched the guard walk past below him.

He inched his way slowly inside the compound through the tree branch. His lean frame moved efficiently to a lower branch which startled an owl sitting on the branch and hooted its annoyance at the intrusion and flew away.

The lone guard on the terrace stopped his walk and looked towards the tree branch from where the owl had flown away. The lone guard on the terrace stood still and peered at the branch from where the owl had created the commotion. For a moment it looked like he would investigate the cause of the disturbance but changed his mind suddenly and continued his walk when there was no further movement from the tree branch. A quick smile flashed across the otherwise grim features of the man silently perched on the tree trunk. He waited a moment more for the Terrace guard to walk away before he carefully slid towards the large balcony on the first floor.

Priyu yawned and massaged his aching neck. He initialed the paper he was reading and pushed it into the top drawer of the desk before locking it. He was a very busy man and he had had a very tiring day. He got up from his desk stretching and extinguished the reading lamp on his table.

He looked at the large lonely bed in his office room. Or is this now my bedroom?, he asked himself. He had been sleeping here more often than his own bed next to his beautiful wife, one floor below. It is too late to go down and disturb her he decided as he changed and got ready for bed.

Priyu had gone to bed with a score of unresolved issues of the Royal state in his mind and had just fallen into a tired asleep on his office bed when he felt the cold breeze of the evening caress his face and thin beard. He opened his eyes sleepily and saw the curtains on his large balcony door which was to his left swaying gently to the breeze. With half open eyes he lazily watched the curtains sway till a frown spread across his shiny forehead and he suddenly sat up straight with a start on his bed.

He reached for his bell that he kept on his bedside but did not ring it looking straight into the shadow of the room.

'Who's there?' he commanded

A shadowy figure wearing dark black and a turban less head slowly emerged from the shadows and stood quietly near the foot of his bed looking intently into the eyes of Priyu.

'Toshin' Priyu sighed and kept down the bell that he had picked up back by the bedside.

The man named Toshin stood still looking at his master Priyu intently as he stood up and took a long gulp of the cool mint water that he kept by his bedside and placed his turban on his head.

'I hate it when you sneak up like that, makes me feel so vulnerable and what happened to your damn turban?' he muttered as he stood up and covered himself with a shawl.

'May be you should fire your guard on the Terrace' Toshin said.

Priyu shot a glance at him 'Do we need to do that?' he asked him.

'It might be wise' Toshin suggested.

'hmmm' Priyu pondered for a while and he picked up the bell that he kept by his bedside and rang it furiously. The head guard followed by two of his deputies' burst into his room ready for action.

'O Deva' the head guard uttered looking aghast from Priyu to Toshin who now had his face covered and had taken a step back into the darker corner of the room, only his silhouette was visible.

The head of Priyu's security guards was a burly large man with a round bearded face and thick curled up moustache. Inspite of his bulk he moved quickly enough when required.

'Master, are you ok?' he managed in his gruff voice keeping his weapon drawn towards the shadowy figure. The head guard was squinting his eyes to have a better look at the man in the shadows.

'Yes, I am ok' Priyu answered sharply 'but what does it say about your security when anyone can walk into my chamber unhindered in the middle of the night?'

The Head guard looked towards his deputies who were stationed outside the Main gate and they were frozen out of fear and astonishment looking at the tall lean figure standing in the shadows with his long hair loose and falling on his shoulders. He looked every bit like the 'Pretatma' stories they had heard.

'Who was guarding the terrace?' Priyu asked angrily, snapping them out of their shock.

'It was me, Master' a 4th guard had joined them and walked in quietly and stood in front of Priyu, his head bent.

'I should put you in the dungeon for your incompetence' Priyu roared.

The guard stood silent with his head bent while the head guard breathed a sigh of relief.

'oh, what the hell' Priyu continued looking at the head guard 'Put him in my stables, he is fit only to work on the horses' he dismissed them.

The dismissed Terrace guard glanced at the still silent silhouette of Toshin as he turned and left the room along with the other guards.

'Close the door, behind you' Priyu ordered the guards 'I do not want to be disturbed'.

When they had left the room and the door was closed he looked at Toshin 'Now, give me the details' he said walking into the adjoining office room and indicating a chair for him to sit down and settled down on the chair in front of him.

2. The Council

2

The Council

It was nearing dawn when Priyu approached the private entrance to the King's palace at a slow pace on horseback. He preferred the horseback ride to the horse drawn carriage which was now increasingly used by the elite. Being on horseback he could feel the warmth of the sun on him and the breeze. There was the strong smell of fresh cow dung being applied on the mud road that lead to the gate. The heavy foliage of the trees that lined both sides of the small street hid the morning light and made it darker than it really was. The birds and the squirrels were chirping their morning tweets and the monkeys were waking up from their slumber and were already creating a racket, but all of this was all lost on Priyu as he was deep in thought as he handed over his horse to the guard. Outwardly he looked calm as usual as he acknowledged the greeting of the guard and waited for the small gate to be opened to allow him entrance to the private chambers of the King.

The conspicuous gate was opened and he was allowed into a small waiting room. There he was greeted by Fouja the Kings General. If a man's life story could be etched on a person's face, Fouja's face told a life of grit, pain and hardship. It was scarred by a hundred battle wounds and these extended to his arms and his grizzled rough hands. Greeting Fouja by the customary two handed hand shake was always an unpleasant task for Priyu. Fouja's palms felt like rubbing hands against a tree bark, except it lacked the warmth of nature.

Fouja looked straight past Priyu as they hurriedly dispensed with this custom and waited for the guards to lead them through the long inner maize of doors, stairs, courtyards and corridors that lead to the King's private receiving chamber.

They walked through gardens, numerous doors and a winding staircase that Priyu had seen for the first time despite his numerous visits to the King's private chambers. Only a handful of the King's personal guards knew these corridors well and each of them took a different route to reach the chambers.

The guard took them to the door and knocked on the door twice for the chamber maid to open the door. A tall striking figure with a thin long face opened the polished ornate door a crack and eyed them appraisingly. Priyu smelled her strong perfume and heard the jingling of her anklets, earrings and various other ornaments she decked herself with before he could make eye contact. Her look of disapproval and dislike was not reflected by Priyu. He did not want to give her the pleasure of knowing that she made him uncomfortable. She lingered behind the door a moment longer than was necessary to make the General impatient and then slowly and dramatically opened the door with an exaggerated bow which also conveyed how taller she was to Priyu and the General.

Priyu and the General walked past her and were surprised to see the young King Smikruta already waiting for them in his receiving room. He was standing by the large window taking in the cool breeze. He turned his head slightly sideways and turned back to look out of the window a little while longer. He took in a deep breath and seemed to be rejuvenated by the fresh air as he turned around to face them. They bowed and greeted the King in their customary 'Hail Almagri' greeting.

The King was in his semi-formal attire. The robe he wore was open up from his waist and was not tied or buttoned up as protocol required when attending official duties. Though Priyu was a little dismayed by this informality from the King he chose to overlook this at the moment but made a mental note to convey this to the King at an opportune moment. Priyu was a master of ceremony and protocol and insisted on protocol and tradition at any cost and most certainly from the King, the highest authority in the Kingdom even when meeting them in his inner most circle. Atleast, he is wearing his Royal turban he consoled himself.

he King seemed fresh and composed even though he had very less sleep last night. Priyu knew this for a fact as they had both sat late last night before Priyu had returned home to more work and no doubt the King had meetings after Priyu had departed.

There was a large wooden table on the right side of the room propped up by four stallions on each corner, but the King preferred to sit on the more comfortable cushioned chairs and sofa like diwan at the far end of the room.

Xyree the chamber maid walked up to them followed by another maid and placed cut fruits, scented water, warm milk and a coffee brew on the center table and she dismissed the other maid and waited by the Kings seat. The King settled down on his chair and Priyu and Fauja followed suit.

'So tell me' the King spoke.

Priyu sat quiet and when the King looked up at Priyu he looked towards Xyree who was still standing near the King. The King waved her away and she pivoted slowly and walked away her pointed sandals clicKing loudly on the white marble floor, her back rigid with dignity.

Priyu avoided looking at her retreating back and studiously studied the lines on his palm till she had exited the room and didn't speak till he heard the click of the door being closed behind her.

Priyu had just opened his mouth to speak, when the door opened again and this time it was a man wearing the most elaborate turban Priyu had ever seen walked in slowly. He wore the turban with a bright red emblem of the Leaping Stallion sticking out prominently.

Priyu and the General Fauja stood up immediately bowing to Prince Brihu the older brother of King Smrikruta as he entered the room. Instead of walking towards them he turned to the life size idol of the Almagri goddess which was behind the Kings table, he saluted her elaborately and gravely, while the others waited for him.

He then turned towards them and walked upto the King and saluted him customarily before taking his seat next to the King.

'So what was so urgent?' he demanded somberly as he took his place next to the King.

'The reports are true, I am afraid' Priyu said addressing both of them, 'I now have confirmation that King Oleva is preparing for battle'

'Haha, that rat Oleva', snorted Prince Brihu leaning forward. 'Has he already forgotten his defeat at my hands?' he said as he reached for the hot brewing kettle of coffee on the table and poured himself a cup full.

Priyu remembered the famous victory of Prince Brihu over King Oleva all too well but he chose to not consider that for now.

'What makes you so sure that Oleva is preparing for war again?' the King asked Priyu.

Priyu knew that this question was asked by the King more for the benefit of his brother than himself or the General.

'As you are aware' Priyu started 'I first had my doubts when we had captured the crew of the ship who were caught near our shores'.

The General shifted uncomfortably in his chair, he was angry that his men were not involved in the seizure of the small ship that had drifted near their border shore line a few months back. Most of the ship's crew had fled when the ship was boarded by the men of the secret services reporting to Priyu. They had managed to capture just one of them, who turned out to be the cook on board the abandoned ship.

What had further infuriated the General was that the prisoner was handed over to his army only when the secret service had interrogated him first. They had got enough information from the prisoner to confirm that they were transporting a large shipment of arms & a new smelly powder which exploded when it was heated.

'Unfortunately we did not get to see what the entire shipment was, we only found some strangely shaped arrows and possibly a bow string. From what little we found, I can say that this has come from some far away land'.

'I have never seen such armament before' the General chipped in. 'This arrow does not fit the typical Bow, it seems a special kind of bow and the arrow is designed to fly a hundred more *hasta than our arrows can fly and their arrow heads can pierce our armour easily'. He said gravely scratching a deep scar on his chin subconsciously.

The King looked at Priyu, 'This arrow you found, what is the metal used? Is it equal to ours?' he asked.

'Close' Priyu answered. 'Our metal has been a well-kept secret, our arrows has been built to break armour for some time now, and we have not shared this with anyone so far. But this arrow seems just as good, if not better' he said.

'What has Sanigya the Chariot Lady got to say about it?' he asked Priyu. The King was referring to the chief armament designer for the Kingdom of Almagri.

'She has seen it and she is testing it' said Priyu 'But unfortunately we don't have a large amount of their metal to melt it and study it'.

'So continuing with my report, once the ship was captured, I sent my spies to the 4 Kingdoms of Oleva, Smarga, Trinu and to Achuta's Kingdom' said Priyu.

'Achuta? You spied on Achuta's Kingdom?' the General said looking at the King and the Prince bewildered 'They are our allies, our King has married his sister to the young Achuta Prince' he exclaimed.

'I know, but better safe than sorry' said Priyu patiently.

The King urged him to continue with his report.

'Even though I had sent my spies to these Kingdoms my suspicion was always with Oleva' he said. 'I lost a man whom I had stationed there long back, in fact we lost the entire family' he said sadly. 'My doubts were strengthened when this happened, that it was not a coincidence that we find their smuggling ship and immediately my spy gets killed there. That could not be mere coincidence. So I sent my best man there a few days back and he just returned last night with his findings'. He stopped and took a sip of strong coffee brew that was poured for him.

'And what is the report?' the impatient General prodded him, sitting on the edge of his chair.

'Whatever the report' Prince Brihu cut in before Priyu could proceed 'Let the fool of a King try again, we will destroy him for good this time' he said already looking bored with the conversation.

'King Oleva has many flaws, but being a fool is not one of them' Priyu said.

'Are you saying that a few strangely shaped arrows and some smelly powder can defeat the mighty Almagri army?' asked Prince Brihu as he leaned over with some trouble and poured some more coffee into his already empty cup.

Priyu sighed and leaned back into his chair crossing his fingers in an intersection and resting it on his chest.

'When I first got reports of his plans to attack us, I could not fathom his reasons for taking such a step' said Priyu 'Why would a man twice defeated by us soundly and humiliated in the last battle try again? How could a Kingdom which is depleted of its past wealth and glory, think of a conquest?' he looked around the room questioningly.

'As the Prince said, he is an arrogant rogue' the General spat out. 'And they have long eyed our port. They cannot reconcile that they have to pay us for the use of the port'.

'Yes that is true, but is it enough reason for him to commit to another war? Is it not cheaper to pay tax than go for war?' asked Priyu.

'So dear Priyu, what makes him confident that he can beat us this time?' the King asked 'Does he have some secret weapon that we do not have?'

Priyu was silent for a while before he could answer '... hmm, you can say that' he said gravely.

'Stop beating around the bush Priyu, what does the fool have that scares you so much?' Prince Brihu asked with a smirk, taking a long sip of the steaming hot brew.

Priyu hesitated speaking out, he turned to look towards the Almagri idol, as if he was seeking her strength and guidance.

'So what is it Priyu?' the King asked softly leaning forward.

The King and the General both looked at Priyu with attention as he spoke.

'As per my reports King Oleva has been seen in the company of a Rohini' he said finally.

There was a stunned silence in the room. Prince Brihu who was about to sip his brew stopped midway, his mouth open.

General Fauja equally shocked blurted out loudly 'What nonsense?' 'The Rohini's are gone. The world has seen the last of them' he continued, 'No, it is not possible. We got rid of the lot…yes each and every one them' he ranted.

King Smrikruta discreetly took the cup of coffee from Prince Brihu's hands which were trembling and he slowly placed his cup back on the table. Priyu pretended that he did not notice this while the General looked like he would launch into another rant any moment now.

'Unfortunately, not all of them are gone' said Priyu. 'Apparently some of them have survived'.

There was a long silence in the room, each of them seemed to absorb this disturbing news in their own way. The King seemed to be deep in thought, while Prince Brihu seemed to have frozen out of fear and the General kept shaking his head as to how it is not possible. The General like most men of action preferred an enemy who would play by the rules of combat, whom he could see, touch, hear and pierce. When it came to the occult and supernatural the General was out of his depth and had no strategy for the unseen enemy.

He mopped the perspiration from his forehead and stood up abruptly. 'Damn this Oleva' he cursed out loudly, stomping about the room. 'Only he can sink this low, the cunning bloodsucker' he roared.

'Relax, Fauja' the King commanded quietly but firmly. There was metal in his voice, his voice clear and strong the one he used to address vast gatherings carried across the vast room easily and stopped Fauja on his tracks and also seemed to wake up the Prince from his stupor as he also straightened up and adjusted his turban.

'I apologise, your majesty' Fauja said 'I am truly sorry, I forgot where I was'.

'No need to apologise' the King spoke calmly 'There is cause for concern, but this is no time to panic. We have not heard fully what Priyu has to say. So resume your seat and let us listen to him first' as he waited for the General and his brother to collect their thoughts, he clapped his hands.

Xyree the chamber maid appeared from the next room almost instantly. The men lost in their thoughts barely noticed her as she glided across with practiced grace. Her long flowing robe slithering around her showing glimpses of her smooth legs almost upto her waist.

She walked tall, straight and regal till she reached their sitting area at the end of the room but upon reaching her Kings side she bent her head down coyly awaiting his instructions.

'Bring us some of that hot special brew of yours' he said.

She complied immediately and produced a shiny brass pot which was studded with semi-precious stones with a long curved spout and poured an aromatic coffee brew into silver cups and handed them to the King, the Prince, Priyu and Fauja.

Once she had done her ceremony she once again awaited for the Kings orders who again waved her away, the General was fidgeting in his chair impatient with the ceremony and gulped down the coffee and set his cup down wiping his beard with the sleeve of his shirt.

Priyu took a sip of his brew and it was the strongest coffee he had ever tasted, he quickly set down the cup.

The King seemed to be considering this calmly as he moved forward in his chair and asked Priyu 'Are you sure about this…this Rohini…I mean this sorceress?' he asked.

He felt his brother wince at the mention of 'Rohini'.

'Yes my lord, unfortunately the news is true' Priyu confirmed 'My man almost killed his horse, riding all night to give me this news' he sighed.

The King gave out a gasp, the stallion was the symbol of his Kingdom and he had a special affinity towards the beast.

'About 3 Yojana* from Tirukutta (Oleva's capital) is the Sarpatta forest. This forest is at the foothills of the Sarpatta Mountain. All kinds of wild beasts and serpents roam the forest and that has kept most people away from even venturing near the forest.

But the last few months a few people in the village near the forest have seen King Oleva and his closest bodyguards enter the forest regularly. The villagers whisper that King Oleva goes there to visit this Rohi....er this sorceress' Priyu spoke. 'She has made the forest her home. Reports are that she has also cured him of the deformity he had on his face.'

Priyu paused and looked at the Prince, the King nodded and encouraged Priyu to continue.

'As you know the purple patch on his face had completely deformed the right side of his face including blinding his right eye. As a result he never showed that side of his face and used to wear a mask to hide that deformity. But now, he no longer wears the golden mask. They also say that he is growing bigger and stronger everyday.

According to my source, this sorceress has given him a special potion that gives any man who drinks it the strength of an ox and the courage of a lion'. He paused for a while and let his words sink in, he continued 'and at the moment there is no easy way to confirm this. But what is confirmed is that they have started war like preparations, he has been sourcing arms and building up stores for weapons. He has bought horses, elephants and slaves. His army has started training regularly and have been practicing formations and strategies. They have also bought Tents, chariots, food stock, grains, tools to dig trenches, ladders etc. It all points to preparation of an attack' he concluded.

'Could this be true?' the King asked deep in thought.

'What could be true?' asked Priyu.

'That they get this superhuman strength from this magic potion?' asked the King.

"The fact that the sorceress is in Sarpatta is true but about the magic potion, I believe much of this is village gossip. One can never be sure of such things your Majesty. No one seems to have actually seen this sorceress. The villagers of Sarpatta say that whoever ventures near the forest never comes back. Children who went to pick dry wood have disappeared and same is true for the goats and cows which were taken to graze there have never returned. And about the magic potion itself even the belief that they have this magic power can demoralize the opposite army and give them a mental edge'.

'True' Fauja said thoughtfully. He poured himself another cup of the strong brew and Priyu noticed with satisfaction that his hands were steady.

'Oleva has always been envious of our shoreline and our port' said the King. 'He has been eyeing this region for a very long time'.

'How long do you estimate before he makes a move?' the General asked.

'From the looks of it, Oleva would be prepared in a couple of fortnights to march' said Priyu.

'How long do we need to prepare ourselves?' the King asked the General.

'Six days' the General answered readily 'Our weapons are ready, we need to get the elephants and horses ready and to set up our defences.'

'Good, start it. I will be sending a messenger to King Achuta, to send a battalion' he said. 'He owes us, after we held off the Kriyu from attacKing them'.

'What are your thoughts?' the King asked Priyu. 'Do you see any chance in negotiating with Oleva? He will not rest until there is a definite end to this issue', the King mused.

The Prince who was quiet all this while spoke out suddenly 'He is a greedy mean bastard, that Oleva' he spat out 'He is a snake in a man's body. We cannot negotiate with snakes'

'I agree' Priyu responded. 'We just cannot trust this Oleva. He has gone back on his words too many times and has tried every sneaky act to get what he wanted'.

'The 'negotiation' is only to buy us some time' the King answered. 'King Achuta will take at least 2 fortnights for his men to get ready and reach here'.

'Why cannot we just rid of Oleva?' the General remarked caressing his rough beard.

'We have a understanding within the 4 Kingdoms, and I am not going to break that accord' the King said emphatically.

'But nothing says we cannot get rid of the sorceress' said Priyu quietly.

The King sat up straight and looked at Priyu, the General stopped scratching his scar and the Prince took in a deep breath as he looked at the King and Priyu.

'What do you propose?' the King asked Priyu.

'As far as the Oleva kingdom goes the sorceress is non-existent, they do not acknowledge her existence, in fact they deny the existence of any of the Rohini's and such.' continued Priyu, 'If we manage to finish her, they cannot raise an issue with the other Kingdoms' he concluded.

'Can this be done? Can you do this?' asked the Prince sitting up straight on the edge of the sofa, speaking with enthusiasm for the first time since Priyu had dropped the news of the sorceress.

'I have thought of something' was the only thing Priyu added, offering no further information.

'Let's say we manage to get rid of this sorceress' the King said 'Would this be enough to deter Oleva from carrying out his attack?' the King pondered.

'That may not stop him but it will be a huge morale booster for our army and a moral victory for us' said Priyu. 'It will also send out a strong message to Oleva to stand down'.

'Yes, that's it' the General clapped his thighs 'let's finish off the Rohini witch, no more magic potion, no more black magic. I hate them'. For the first time in the meeting he and the Prince were breathing easily.

'But who will do it?' the General said suddenly out loud looking at the King and towards Priyu.

'That is what I was thinking too' the King said looking at Priyu. He had a pretty good idea of what Priyu was about to say but asked him nevertheless.

'What do you say to this Priyu? I would like your men to carry out this mission.'

'Yes, I will use my men' said Priyu, allowing it to be the King's decision.

All the men in the room except for Priyu breathed out a sigh of relief. Priyu was in deep thought as the King called out to the relief of the General and the Prince 'Shall we conclude the meeting then?'

'This sorceress…' the Prince spoke hesitantly dreading to find out the answer 'Could it be the same one?' he managed to say at last.

'No, I very much doubt it' Priyu said to the visible relief of the Prince. Priyu had spoken with a conviction he knew was not true. There was no way for Priyu to know at the moment who she was or was not, but it would save the Prince some sleepless nights he considered.

Priyu stood up along with the General who stood up a little too eagerly. They both bowed to the King awaiting his dismissal. 'Priyu, please stay behind. There is another matter that needs discussion' he said to him as Priyu nodded and remained standing.

He now turned to the General, 'A word of caution' he said. 'You have to make your preparation nevertheless but discreetly. We do not want to warn them we are aware of their intentions'.

'Yes your Majesty' said Fauja. 'You can trust me on this your Majesty, we will be prepared for all eventuality, but I will pray to the Sun god and to the almighty goddess Almagri that it does not come to that' he said bowing to the King and Prince Brihu.

Turning to Priyu he said 'I wish you success' before exiting the room.

It was now the turn of the Prince who moved to Priyu and clasped Priyu's hand tightly 'May Goddess Almagri guide you and your men and give you success' he said. He bowed to the King and the idol of the goddess as he made his way out of the room. The King and Priyu both noticed that the Prince limped visibly as he walked out of the room.

They both watched him leave with concern. When they were alone the King turned and walked towards the window as Priyu followed him. He looked out of the window at the city of Almagri and the lush green hills beyond as he breathed in the beauty of the visual in front of him. It seemed to calm him as the King removed his Royal Turban and let his curly long hair loose with a tired sigh.

'Ah these damn turbans' he cursed, massaging his neck. 'Last night I had the strangest of dreams', he said. 'I was walking towards a waterfall. It was the most beautiful waterfall I have seen, there was a rainbow formed near it and the pool around it was blue and beautiful. There were colourful fishes swimming in the shallow water, colourful birds and beasts like I have never seen before. But they were all silent, mute, not a whisper or sound from any of them. As I neared it the water started roaring, It was angry and it got hotter and hotter and

I realized it was not a waterfall at all but a big flaming fire. It was a huge mountain of fire and it was devouring everything in its path' he stopped. 'What do you make of this dream?' he asked Priyu.

Priyu was thoughtful for a while 'Has it ever happened that you have had a bad dream and that has followed up by some misfortune?' asked Priyu.

'Not that I remember' said the King 'Do you think I should consult Archika on this?' he asked.

'In this matter he would be the right person to consult, your Majesty' said Priyu making a mental note to stop by Archika's house on his way back.

Archika was the Kings personal astrologer and advisor and the King greatly listened to his advice and counsel. Archika also happened to be the brother of Priyu's wife and Priyu enjoyed a mutually respectful relationship with Archika, they understood each other well.

'We cannot do it officially, you understand? I could not use Fauja's men for this mission' he said changing the subject, he was serious and alert now.

'Yes, I do understand your Majesty' Priyu assured him.

'They should not trace it back to our Kingdom. What happens if by chance your men are captured?'

'They will never open their mouths. This I guarantee, they would rather cut their tongues than betray you and our Kingdom, your Majesty', said Priyu.

'You are the only man I can depend upon completely. The Kingdom needs you now more than ever Priyu' said the King placing his hands on Priyu's shoulders. He towered over the diminutive Priyu.

Priyu bowed his head and bid farewell to the King as he slowly backed away from the King and made his way to the exit where the Kings guard awaited to escort him back.

The moment Priyu exited his private chamber, Xyree walked in. She glided in smoothly her long flimsy robe swaying effortlessly to the cool morning breeze. The King had now moved to the long sofa like diwan.

'It is quite cold your Majesty' Her voice was strangely masculine.

'hmmm' the King muttered absentmindedly studying her figure from her darkly coloured lips all the way down to her feet as she stood in display in front of him. She had struck a pose similar to the pose of the idol she had seen carved on the Palli temple that stood at the center of their town.

It was a bold confident pose inviting the onlooked to have a unobstructed view of her body. Her right hand lay easily by the side of her hips and with her left hand she casually toyed with the locks of her hair that fell on her bosom. The King regarded her quietly lying down on the diwan.

'Do you have that magic oil of yours?' he asked

'Of course My Lord' she said as she produced a small glass cut vial from the inner recesses of her cloths and poured a drop on her fingertips and she held her fingers near him to smell it.

The King took a deep breath of the scent and closed his eyes resting his head on the curved end of the diwan.

She poured a few more drops on her fingertips and moved her fingers slowly through his hair and forehead massaging his head expertly as the King sighed and loosened his body. She began murmuring a lullaby in her foreign language and strange accent. He had no idea what she was singing but her usually masculine voice now had a softness and was soothing as he drifted off to a tired sleep.

3. Oleva

3

Oleva

She bent over the wooden bowl, her left breast was hanging loose out of the coarse leather garment she wore. She squeezed it and a stream of milk jutted out and collected in the bowl. She carried the bowl of milk to a clay pot and scooped up a thick glue like substance from the clay pot and added it to the milk. She then added a thumb full of white powder from a small box and mixed it into the bowl along with the milk solution and the milk acquired a bluish hue. She signaled the hulking giant who was standing by the door hunched and transfixed by the exposed breast.

She snapped her finger at him and he looked up laboriously at her and recognition seemed to dawn on his face.

'Feed this to Kulgi' she ordered pushing the bowl towards him as he slowly lumbered towards her. He had to part rough matted hair from his thick large forehead to look at her and extended his huge palm. His palms where the size of a lotus leaf as it engulfed the bowl that she had placed in his extended palm.

She looked at the dull eyes of the giant and said slowly 'This is for Kulgi, you understand?'

He looked at the bowl in his hands and at her.

'Not for you, you thick oaf' though the words were harsh she spoke smoothly enjoying the confusion of the giant. She had not bothered to cover her breast as it hung loosely from her garments.

He grunted in answer and turned and shuffled his way out of the room looking for Kulgi.

Kulgi the black leopard was waiting for her bowl of magic milk on her favourite tree branch directly in front of the ramshackle dwelling from where the giant emerged. Her long tail was twitching in anticipation as she smelled the giant first and then the magic milk as he emerged from the door.

Kulgi and the giant shared a mutual distrust as she watched him with what looked like cool detachment but her senses were heightened when she saw the walking banquet of meat and bones approach her. Over the recent years she had developed a taste for human meat. Instinct had always trained her to avoid humans and she had been successful in doing so till this strange being had come to live right in the middle of the forest with her human giant of a pet. This strange being had captured her and instead of killing her, had fed her the magic milk which Kulgi had now grown accustomed to. This strange being though looked, walked and talked like a human did not smell like a human at all and Kulgi had developed a healthy fear of this being.

But the giant was a different matter altogether and she was finding it increasing difficult to not view the giant as fair game.

She yawned as he neared her showing her large canines and waited majestically spread out till he was directly underneath her.

'What a fool' she thought 'I could crush his stupid skull easily and he is dumb enough to turn his back on me, but even this idiot has his use for now'.

The Giant placed the bowl near the tree and straightened slowly, in his right hand he had his dagger concealed which he held on to tightly under the dirty layers of rags that he wore.

He looked up and looked straight into the yellowish piercing eyes of the black cat. 'Someday this dagger will be twisted deep into your black heart and before you die I will pluck out your piss coloured eyes and I will see how arrogant you are then' he thought.

He turned his back again defiantly and paused a moment. He heard the low rumble of her disapproved growl as her tail twitched stiffly her ears were straight. He walked slowly away the dagger ready and ears straining for the slightest rustle to turn around. His heart pounding slowed down only when he entered the dwelling and closed the heavy wooden door behind him in relief.

He wiped the beads of sweat that had collected on his forehead as he stealthily spied her from the small window.

Kulgi hopped down lightly from the branch in which she was majestically perched a moment ago to the bowl and lapped up the milk lustily. The giant's breathing quickened as he saw the transformation taking place in front of eyes. Kulgi was coming for her magic milk far too frequently now. What was once a fortnightly affair had turned into twice or even thrice a week now.

The moment she drank the milk her powerful limbs seemed to lose its strength and she sunk to the floor panting hard. He could hear her grunt and her powerful exhalation seemed to carry all the way towards him from her prone position. Her grunting and panting grew stronger, faster and louder till it reached a crescendo and then it stopped all of a sudden.

There was a dead silence and eeriness all around the slumped form of Kulgi. Even the breeze seemed to stop blowing, the tree had stopped swaying and was still, so were the birds and the giant who was watching her closely his nose almost outside the window bars. Kulgi had stopped moving all together, she was not breathing, her eyes were tightly shut and she looked like a worn out bit of black rug cast away.

Then the change happened, there was the involuntary shudder as her hair stood straight as she growled and opened her eyes looking straight into the giants eyes. Kulgi's eyes were no longer the piss coloured yellow the giant detested, it now shone a deep green hue that terrified the giant and was frozen in his spot even as he tried to take a step back. He was glad that there was a thick door separating him from this cursed beast. Before he could react she was up and was facing the giant in her crouching stance. She seemed to be getting bigger each time she drank the potion. Her head seemed rounder and her shoulders seemed much more muscular. She stood straight and looked straight into the giant's eyes filled with hate and loathing and then before he could blink she was gone. She shot off like a flash into the bushes and out of site. The giant finally drew out a sigh and relaxed his grip on the dagger.

From her room, lying on her back she watched the discomfort of the giant with a sense of bored curiousness. She was lying down on her mattress of animal skins with her legs perched high on the wall. She was looking at the giant from an inverted position with her dark long locks of hair cascading to the ground from her platform which also served as her bed. Her long almond shaped face was dangling below the bed as she lay loosely on the heap of animal skins.

She curled up her legs and made a reverse flip to land smoothly on her feet. She moved with animalistic litheness and effortlessness as she slithered rather than walked to the room inside and disrobed. There was a tub of warm water set in the middle of the room. She poured in a strong smelling potion in it and got into the tub of water.

''Oleg'' the giant heard her voice call to him. The voice was in his head than something she had said aloud. He turned around and moved slowly into the room where she was in the tub. He stopped as he entered the room, right next to her bath tub was the dreaded lizard that come and went as it pleased. This lizard was as big as his arm. They contemplated each other silently for a brief moment then it turned and left through the window from which it had come in. He turned to the bath tub and he could see only the top of her dark head, the rest of her was submerged in water.

The rest of her face emerged slowly from the water and she rested contentedly against the tub sighing and looking pleased with herself. The Giant peered closely at her, she seemed different.

Her dark shaggy long locks of hair now looked soft, shiny and straight and her coarse skin looked soft and glowing but the most striking change was in her eyes. Her usual slanted slit eyes now looked larger rounder and brighter, they even matched her dark hair.

'We are having a visitor' she whispered. He blinked at her, her thin dark red lips had hardly moved but the voice was very clear in his ears. 'Bring out that wine and crystal here' she pointed to the small bronze table besides her tub.

The giant looked out of the window as he moved out of the room, he saw no one but did not bother asking her who was coming and just ambled towards the kitchen.

King Oleva and his bodyguards moved slowly through the thick foliage; he could sense the discomfort of his mount as it moved ahead reluctantly. His guards and the King were in full battle armor. Their spears drawn, eyes and ears straining for the smallest movement and sound.

The King had his arm on his sword and was just as alert as his guards and they relaxed a little only when they reached the open clearing that led to the sorceress's dwelling in the forest.

To the outsider it looked like an abandoned shack, there was no smoke from the chimney, no light, no human chatter, clothes or utensils to be seen. Only the stench of rotting meat and dried skin gave it an ominous uninviting character. Any traveler or lost soul if he was unfortunate enough to stumble upon this shack would have preferred to brave the dangers of the forest than risk entering this foreboding dwelling.

King Oleva and his guards on the other hand were relieved to see the dwelling and enter its clearing and remain in its vicinity. Even the most fearless of the Kings guards were uneasy in the forest inhabited by the dreaded Kulgi who was fast gaining a notorious reputation as a fearsome beast that preyed on the village cattle and had even turned maneater. To make matters worse Kulgi had now started killing for fun. On one particular night she had brazenly entered the village cow shed and had slaughtered all the cows in a night of mayhem and bloodshed. Kulgi had also taken up to carrying off children and anyone to dared to stray into her domain.

The hunting party organized by the villagers had ended disastrously for the villagers as Kulgi's viciousness and lust for blood had now attained mythical proportions. The terrorized village had organsied a hunting party of 7 villagers who had braved to go after Kulgi in a fit of desperation.

They were all decimated save one, who survived to tell the gory tale of the monstrous Kulgi with green eyes and the savagery of a dozen lions. It had torn through the net which had captured her as though it was cotton and had attacked the unlucky hunters. It had pretended to have fallen prey to the hunters trap but it was the hunters who were hunted by the indomitable Kulgi who had lured the hunters into a false sense of security when they had seen her trapped in the net that had engulfed her. The moment the hunters had relaxed their guard Kulgi had torn through the net and had attacked the hunting team in a flash. The lone survivor had fled with a torn limb and had jumped into the fast flowing Aruyi river that had carried him downstream.

The villagers believed that Kulgi was the devil incarnate and were increasingly agitating against the King for not taking any action against the demon cat. The reluctance of the King to organize a hunting party had angered the villagers and they had demanded protection for man and cattle from the ever increasing boldness of Kulgi.

The heavy wooden door of the dwelling opened and the giant stood at the entrance dwarfing the King and the guards who were one of the biggest and the strongest in the Kingdom, yet they looked like little children against the bulk of the giant who grunted at them with dislike. He stepped aside for the King to enter the dwelling and to the dismay of the guards closed the door behind the King and ambled over to a shed next to the dwelling and sat down on the straw. He was immediately accosted by a large squirrel that jumped upon him and perched on his shoulder. The giant bellowed out laughing and dug into his pocket and pulled out a fist full of sunflower seeds and began feeding his pet squirrel.

The guards looked at each other quizzingly and chuckled amoung themselves mocking the giant and his pet squirrel.

King Oleva moved into the dwelling and was always surprised as to how the dwelling looked larger on the inside than what seemed to be suggested from the outer appearance. He stood in the large circular room with the only source of light was from a dirty glass skylight dome in the centre of the slanting roof. The musty light that filtered in fell on a raised platform in the center of the room like a spotlight. A few animal skins were strewn around on the platform. There were containers made of glass and metal strewn across a large crude wooden table and all over the room. Despite the mess and the stench outside, the room itself did not smell musty or stale. This circular room led to a few more rooms behind the raised platform.

He sniffed hard and followed the smell of lilacs to the chamber in which stood a white marble tub in the center of the room. He stood at the entrance of the room and surveyed it before entering it. This chamber had a softer touch in contrast to the crudeness and filth of the main room. The floor was of compressed soil and felt soft to walk on, he felt as though he was walking into a large cave.

'My Knight in Shining Armour' she cooed from the bath tub. She had her hair piled up high in a bun and the candles lit around the room gave a golden hue that seemed to make her skin look smoother and silkier. She smiled at him alluringly inviting him in.

'It's a pleasant surprise, my King' she said 'I was not expecting you for another full moon atleast'.

'Your bloody cat…that Kulgi' he muttered surveying her as she raised herself from the tub and walked towards him.

'Here let me help you with this' she said smoothly as she turned him around and started unbuckling his heavy armour.

'We have to talk' he turned around brusquely and walked to a coarse wooden chair set against the wall and sat down heavily and uncomfortably on it.

'Do something about that damn cat of yours, if she goes on I will be forced to send a hunt party after her' he said in his grating rough voice. 'I believe the farmers have already given out a reward to anyone to can capture or kill her' he rasped.

'Oh, don't you worry about Kulgi, she can take care of herself'.

'I don't care for your damn Kulgi, I wish that pest was dead myself. I have lost 2 of my best men to her' he spat out. His voice raising with every syllable.

She moved smoothly over to him and knelt down close to him studying his face minutely. Her silky smooth porcelain skin shone like polished white marble. Up close she looked extraordinarily delicate and fragile without a blemish or a wrinkle on her smooth carved features in contrast to the coarse and blunt features of King Oleva.

Her dark almond shaped eyes looked deeply into the eyes of the King and he seemed to relax a bit. She caressed his large rough face soothingly and studied the pale blue patch on the right side of his face which was once a festering dark purple patch. It has since subdued to a very light pale blue tint and was diminishing fast.

She moved her fingers delicately over the scar and looked deep into his right eye which once blind and white now had faint traces of green in them.

King Oleva stood up abruptly as though he had come out of a trance and realized that he was out of his armour and his garments. He now stood facing her, a head taller than her and just as wide. She stayed closed to him and moved her hand tracing the light blue patch all the way from his face to his neck, shoulder and down to his chest. The once purple mark had softened in colour but the new skin that had grown in its place was turning rough and coarse.

'hmm, its healing well' she muttered feeling the texture of the new skin that had grown on his wound.

'Healing well?' he roared. 'Just look at it' he said, anger, irritation and confusion written all his face 'what is that thing?'

'It's a work in progress, my King' she said backing a little away from him so that she could survey him fully.

'But do you see, what I am seeing?' she asked smoothly

'What is it? What are you seeing?'

'I am seeing a man who no longer has to hide his face behind a mask. I am seeing a man who has gained the strength of a dozen men'.

'But I am unable to sleep at night' said the troubled King. 'My head is constantly aching and my skin is always itching. Nothing is making me feel better' he growled.

'Small price to pay, my lord' she said as she moved closer and caressed his big hairy heaving chest. 'Won't it be worth the trouble when you see his head at your feet? The head of the man who gave you this wound?'

The agitated King took in a deep breath and looked at her 'But when?' he asked 'My army is ready to march, when will my men get that damned potion?'

'When the time is right, my lord' she answered reassuringly. 'Your men will be ready to move to battle soon. They will be just as strong and just as fearless as you…soon'.

The King allowed himself to be led to the bath tub.

'As far as your headache is concerned, let me see what I can do about that' the King heard her soft voice in his head as he drifted off to sleep in the warm scented water of the bath tub.

4. Archika

4

Archika

Priyu liked walking to Archika's house. The house was in a busy neighbourhood and not many people gave notice to this slight man as he walked the busy street of Almagri on foot like a commoner. Priyu liked to hear snatches of conversation on street corners or sample prices and quality of the produce being sold in shops along the way. The house had an open courtyard right in the center of the house which hosted many a scholars and thinkers to come and debate topics varying from science, astronomy, maths, philosophy to current events. Today was no different as Priyu entered the house the maid escorted Priyu to a small room which was Archika's work room and library, it also gave direct view to the courtyard where Archika was holding court to a group of men and a lone woman who from their attire and mannerisms looked like scholars. They were discussing something animatedly and judging from the number of cups and plates in front of them, this discussion has been going on for a while.

Priyu settled down in a reading chair and picked up a book lying on Archika's table nearby and was trying to make sense of the diagrams and charts in it when he felt a familiar hand on his shoulder.

'I didn't know you were coming here', said Priyu not having to look at the person who had placed her hand on his shoulder.

'You are getting old dear' his wife said as she placed a cup of coffee on the table.

'Umm thank you my dear, I dearly need that' said Priyu hurriedly reaching for the cup taking a sip of the coffee.

'Why do you drink it if you detest it so much' she questioned a smiling Priyu.

'Even if he's King, what goes in your stomach is your business. Just refuse his coffee next time' she advised him.

'And what is this business of me getting older?' Priyu countered changing the topic.

'You forgot, today is Bhrata, I told you yesterday that I was coming here' said Praveena as she sat on the chair near him.

'Oh yes' said Priyu not really recalling the conversation with her.

'You have been working too hard, I believe you had another visitor late last night' she complained as Priyu sipped the coffee made to perfection, no doubt by his wife Praveena. She knew exactly how he liked his coffee and so many little things which he had not cared to express aloud but still she had understood his likes and dislikes without the words being spoken. He studied the elegant woman sitting next to him.

'I should pay more heed to her' he reminded himself 'remember you are the lucky one here'. He recalled the first time he had laid eyes on her. She was all of fifteen and was playing the Veena on the last day of the Vahini utsav. This honour of performing on the last day as a finale to the ceremony was reserved for the maestro's and pandits who had mastered their vocals and instruments of choice. She was by far the youngest recipient of this opportunity to perform before the King's court and visiting dignitaries. Priyu, a young man of 19 then a junior aid in the Kings court had fallen in love with the grace and poise of the young proponent of the Veena. This slight nondescript youth had walked up to her father the following week and had asked for her hand in marriage. Her father had seen the fierce passion and ambition in this young man's eyes and had wisely understood this young man was more than the sum total of his bits.

She on her part was adamant that she would not marry this nobody, even though he had rosy recommendations and promise of a bright future. She had only relented when her father had threatened to take up Sanyas (live a life of renouncement) if she had refused. She had accepted the marriage defeated by her father's threat, but had given up playing the Veena and had steadfastly refused playing it ever since. It had taken her a few years to get accustomed to this strange quiet man and gradually develop a feeling of mutual respect and admiration for his keen brain and sense of purpose in life.

Priyu's train of though was interrupted by the appearance of Archika, who stormed into the room and slammed a bunch of papers on the table.

Priyu and Praveena watched in amusement as Archika stomped about the room 'Intellectuals….bah' he spat out.

'The one thing, they do well……no, no…the only thing they do is talk…talk…and talk.'

'Do they want a solution, no sir and do they even *know* how to find a solution?' he laughed out, 'No…they wouldn't know what a solution is if I stuffed one down their throat.'

He stopped to catch his breath and take a sip of water. This gave a momentary pause to his monologue as he looked at them as though he was just aware of their presence.

'hmmp Bratha' he announced to know one in particular.

'I was wondering what brought you out of that palace of yours to this humble dwelling' he continued in as he reaching to pick a sweet laddu that was on a tray help by Praveena.

'Sit' commanded Praveena, slapping his hand away.

Archika grudgingly took his seat as Praveena applied the sandalwood paste on his forehead and blessed him. 'Open your mouth' she commanded as she placed the sweet laddu in his mouth and was out of the room.

'mmm delicious' munched Archika as he reached for the plate left behind by his sister and offered one to Priyu, which he declined and Archika helped himself to a second laddu.

'So brother' he said between mouthful 'Are you coming here directly from the palace?' he asked as Priyu nodded.

'What is it?' he asked.

'The King and the Prince will consult on you a matter, I want you to be prepared' said Priyu.

'Prepared…hmm' repeated Archika still munching, thoughtfully now.

'The King has been bothered by some dreams that he's been having lately' said Priyu.

'And that bothers you?'

'I don't want a bothered King, now' said Priyu flatly.

'Now?' Archika raised an eyebrow, but when he did not get an answer from Priyu, he continued '…and our Prince? What troubles him?'

'Past deeds' replied Priyu.

'You will have to narrow that one for me' suggested Archika.

'Rohini' said Priyu.

Archika put down the third laddu he had picked and stared at Priyu.

5. Toshin & Dhyum

5

Toshin & Dhyum

The shoal of fish swam in a loose formation, darting easily from one direction to another. They swam closer to inspect a strange creature amidst their corner of the lake. They swam around this motionless figure inspecting it and decided it was not food or foe and after a while their curiosity satisfied they swam off leaving the young man in deep meditation alone.

The young man submerged in the lake focused only on his breathing as he exhaled out slowly, very very slowly. It took him almost as much time as a candle takes to burn out for one solitary exhalation of his breath. His heartbeat had almost come to a stand-still and he had learnt the art of controlling the pace of his heartbeat by the art of deep meditation. The young man meditating sitting fully submerged in the lake was the lone guard on the terrace of Priyu, who was dismissed from his guard duty just a few days back. His name was Dhyum.

The Sakhya's were an aloof band of monks, who looked like and were mostly treated like vagabonds in their rag tags and lack of any wordly possession. They barely spoke or interacted with anyone outside their own small sect and even within themselves they spoke only in syllables when required. No one took much interest in them and neither did they.

They lived off the land and travelled, ate and slept as they pleased. He had come across them as a young boy on one of his forays into the forest to hunt rabbits for their pelts. He had come across them sleeping peacefully in the forest. He had sat and watched them sleep on the moist forest floor feeling no discomfort. The insects, the bugs and the rodents did not seem to bother them one bit. All of them awakened simultaneously and wordlessly started walking together. He had been intrigued and been drawn to their sense of tranquility and calm. They had neither welcomed him nor discouraged him when he started walking alongside them. They just accepted him wordlessly and he travelled and lived with them for 4 years, learning to live off the forest, the secrets of the herbs and plants for their medicinal value and most importantly their art of extreme inward focus and meditation.

The Sakhya's were on a lifelong quest to master the self and shared their knowledge only within their own sect from generation to generation. They could regulate their body temperature, pulse and the senses to an extraordinary level. There were Sakhya's who could even control the growth of their hair, nails and go for days without food. They could walk through snow with no footwear and barely a loincloth and regulate their body temperature to a degree that they could burn you by a mere touch of their finger-tips.

Dhyum had roamed with them till one day they had reached the foothills of mount Prayagh. They had stopped at a small town near the foothills. The town was busy as the last of the pilgrims were leaving the shrine near the foothill of the mountain. It was the onset of winter and the snow had already covered the mountain range in a blanket of mesmerizing bright white monotony. It shone so bright that it hurt the eye to look at it for long. Dhyum was already feeling the chill and had covered himself as best as he could from the what discarded cloth and skin he had found but his fellow travelers seemed to not notice the biting cold. Soon the snow would cover the roads to the mountain range and it would remain closed for the next 5-6 months.

They were walking to take a dip in the holy Prayagh river when Dhyum came across a group of excited kids circled around a little pup in the town square. Dhyum had ventured into the circle to investigate and had found a pup barely a few days old, its tail was tied with a string and the bigger of the kids was dragging it around. The confused scared pup was squeaking and crying out its protest. A few elders sat by looking indifferently as the gang of kids bullied the pup. Dhyum could not resist when he stepped in and snatched the string from the boy and picked up the little pup.

'Let the kids have their fun' one of the men smoking a chillum said impassively to Dhyum while the others remained indifferent squatting and smoking.

When Dhyum did not relent, the boy from whom he had snatched the pup faced upto Dhyum and spoke with defiance 'Its mother has killed our goat. We have already killed its mother and now he will die anyway'.

Dhyum lifted the pup and examined it closely turning it around. It had a thick grey and white coat and he realized that this was no dog, it was a mountain wolf. Dhyum held on to the wolf pup as he walked towards the watching Sakhya group. He walked up to them and they all turned wordlessly towards the river. Dhyum felt a strange awkwardness walking with them, it was for the first time he felt that he was not a Sakhya.

They had finished their dip and had started walking towards the snow clad mountain when they stopped at a fork on the road. They all turned and looked towards Dhyum standing in a circle around him.

He had realized that his journey with them had come to an end now. The eldest of the Sakhya had walked over to young Dhyum and placed both his palms over Dhyum's eyes when the rest of them closed in and placed their palms on his head. Dhyum had closed his eyes and felt a wave of tingling sensation course through his body. He soared up out of his body and looked down upon himself being surrounded by the Sakhya monks, chanting in unison. He was weightless and free as he drifted off. He had no idea how long he had stood there with his eyes closed, when he had opened his eyes they were no longer there. The little pup was asleep in his arms.

Dhyum opened his eyes and looked around him. A boutique of colourful sea life surrounded him. Small fishes of various hues and stripes swam serenely around him. He exhaled the last bit of air out of his lungs and made the short ascent to the surface of the river in which he had spent the better half of the morning.

As he emerged from the river he saw the familiar Grey and White face of his mountain wolf waiting for him on the river bank. It was a fully grown wolf, solidly built. It reflected many of his master's quiet, strong characteristics. Dhyum walked up to the wolf and patted him as the wolf stood up and looked attentively at his master. Laid out on the ground on a large mat neatly arranged were an array of weapons.

There were a number of swords with intricate designs and springs. There was the long sword, two handed double edged swords, daggers, spears, short bows, long bows, cross bows with a spring loaded mechanism and a flexible coiled long sword which was rolled up into a bundle.

He knelt down in front of the weapons and said a short prayer. He picked up the Coiled weapon and unleased the sword in a wide arc. When unfurled the sword hissed like an angry cobra and looked just as deadly. It was spiked on both ends and the flexible blades hissed and swished as Dhyum wielded it expertly in arcs, moving in tandem with the moment of the razor sharp blades. The speed of blades were just a blur and Dhyum continued in this frantic pace for a while till he slowed down gradually and in one flick of his wrists the blades rolled up neatly in a roll and it was no bigger than a human fist. He laid down the coiled weapon carefully.

His ears picked up a high pitched call from a hawk circling high above. The call from the hawk was at such a high frequency that the untrained human ear would not have heard it. He picked up a short dagger with one smooth move as he turned around and faced the woods with the dagger concealed in his arms. He heard the low rumble of Doree his mountain wolf.

'Yes, I hear him' said Dhyum softly.

They both faced the thick forest foliage as a shadowy tall figure stepped noiselessly out from the trees and stood facing Dhyum and Doree.

Doree was off in a flash and raced towards the still figure. Doree the wolf reached the motionless figure and pounced on him forcing him to fall back on the impact of the large wolf on him. Doree rolled with the fallen Toshin licking his face and neck and prancing around him in unbridled joy and love.

Toshin equally jubilant patted and scratched the wolf's ear and neck as Doree purred like a little pup and lapped up all the attention that Toshin was showering on him.

Dhyum had packed up his weapon rucksack and sat down serenely by the river waiting for the duo to join him.

'You're not giving him enough attention' Toshin remarked as he joined Dhyum by the lake side and sat next to him facing the river.

Doree was still delirious over the arrival of Toshin among their midst but toned down her enthusiasm when Toshin sat down by Dhyum's side. But he laid down his head on Toshin's lap and was content being petted by him when the two of them spoke.

'Are you not going to thank me?' Toshin asked

'For what?' asked Dhyum

'For getting you fired from that job, guarding his terrace' said Toshin smiling.

'Doree, you master is very ungrateful man' said Toshin to Doree as Doree looked attentively from Toshin to Dhyum.

Dhyum was silent as he looked out at the glistering river in front of him, 'What is the mission?' he asked eventually.

'You better hear it from Priyu' answered Toshin getting somber himself.

Dhyum looked up at the circling hawk and spoke, 'I think he has reached'.

6. The Mission

6

The Mission

Priyu stopped at the hillock and looked down lovingly at the landscape spread in front of him. It was a clear warm day and there was not a cloud in the sky that cast a shadow on the vast endless carpet of green that was spread in front of him. In the distance he could see the river sparkling with the sun rays bouncing off the calm river. The river widened and curved out of sight behind the hills.

He could see his farmhouse which housed his stable and an orchard and stopped a while to admire the beauty of the picture in front of him.

'It would be a shame to lose this lovely land to that brute Oleva' he thought. 'He would probably start by carving out this very hillock for the granite underneathh'. This thought made him push his mount the sturdy Pari towards his farmhouse.

As he neared the farmhouse he saw the solidly built pair of Toshin and Dhyum waiting for him near the entrance gate of the estate. For a moment he was envious of the youth, vitality and beauty of the pair. Toshin was tall and lanky, athletically built and carried himself in a lazy elegance. He was loose limbed and casual and at times he slouched. He gave the impression of being bored or inattentive, but Priyu knew him better than to get fooled by his casualness. Dhyum a hair shorter than Toshin was a picture of calm and serenity. Though he did not exhibit an overtly muscular frame he was just as if not more athletic than Toshin. He made no unnecessary gestures or conversation. He stood still without being awkward or stiff and was silent usually without looking out of place. He brought about a sense of calmness and easiness to any company he was in without saying a word.

Priyu's mind went back to the business in hand and sobered up at the thought of sending these fine young men on this dangerous mission. He slowed down his horse's gait and hesitated for a brief moment before pressing on with the unpleasant but important task at hand.

Dhyum stepped forward and handled the bridle of Priyu's mount and allowed him to dismount. Priyu was relieved to see that Dhyum had wisely kept his mountain wolf out of sight. He was nervous in the presence of the mighty beast even though he was sure he had nothing to be worried about. Priyu who prided on his poker face wondered if Dhyum had perceived that the wolf made him nervous, this only strengthened his conviction that he had groomed the right person.

No greetings and small talk was required as he dismounted and silently made his way to his farm house followed by Toshin and Dhyum. Once they were seated in the open verandah overlooking the river, Priyu got straight to the point.

'I believe Toshin has given you the back story?' he asked Dhyum impassively and in his best business like tone.

When Dhyum nodded, Priyu continued 'The threat to our Kingdom and way of living is real. Oleva has tried every means to stamp his authority over us but we have managed to thwart him off each time, yet he grows bolder and more desperate'.

'Should we not find a permanent solution for this?' asked Toshin.

They were all seated on a mattress spread on the wooden floor of the verandah. The gentle breeze from the mountain was cool and refreshing.

Priyu closed his eyes 'Alas, I hope our integrity and our adherence to do the right thing will not prove to be our undoing'.

'Is it not the right thing to save our nation and our people from his motives? When they have no regard for the treaty and has broken it time and again, why don't we have the right to defend our lands and our lives? It is time we wage an all-out war against them and finish them once and for all' declared an animated Toshin.

Priyu looked towards the river flowing rhythmically in the distance and smiled at Toshin. 'Do you know how our Kingdom was named?' he asked.

'Yes' volunteered Toshin, 'It was named after the goddess Almagri'.

'And do you know how it came about to be named after the goddess Almagri?' he asked.

When he was met with silence, Priyu continued 'Legend has it that, when King Tishani the great grandfather of our present King was ruling the Kingdom, it was at the height of its power. He had expanded our Kingdom far into the eastern and northern frontiers, capturing and defeating anyone who did not surrender. It was also a time for great trade and commerce and the Kingdom was very wealthy and he had built many a splendorous monuments, parks and temples to celebrate his accomplishments and our city was known to be the most beautiful city of its time, but do you know our kingdom was called then?" he paused for their response.

'It was called Mahimya', it was Dhyum who answered.

'Right' said Priyu 'Mahimya also means Glorious or Wonderful. It was during this time that a very young slave girl amoung many other slaves were brought here to the Kingdom. Her beauty and intelligence was so much beyond her years that, it came to the attention of the King himself.

The King summoned this young girl and ordered her to stay in the palace as a playmate and companion to the young Princess who was as old as the young slave girl whose name was…..Almagri'.

'Now this little slave girl Almagri soon become the confidant and aid of the Princess and they would often take long walks and play games. King Tishani's love for his little daughter was well known throughout the Kingdom and it was for this reason that an evil scheme was being hatched by one of the defeated Kings to kidnap the Princess to avenge his loss. So they laid a trap on one of their walks to the nearby forest and tried to snatch the Princess. When the young slave girl

Almagri who was 12 years of age then realized this, she quickly snatched the Princess's royal emblem and wore it on her head and fought the kidnappers bravely giving time for the Princess to escape and alert the palace guards. The kidnappers carried away the young girl thinking that she was the Princess.

They found her a day later near the edge of the forest mortally wounded and nearing her death. The King took the young dying girl on his lap and asked her if he could do anything for her. "Yes, your majesty" she answered him feebly "Make this Kingdom the most beautiful Kingdom in the word and I would like to be reborn here" she said.

"What more must I do to make it more beautiful?" the King asked her.

"A land is beautiful when all the citizens are free to live their life the way they choose to live, where the citizens love their rulers and not fear them. The land of the Free is the most beautiful Kingdom in the world".

The King understood her message and asked forgiveness from the dying girl and promised her that he will try to make this Kingdom the most beautiful one in the world.

Priyu's eyes had turned moist as he recounted the story of his ancestral land. He took in a deep breath and was silent for a moment.

'You see Toshin and Dhyum, this is what makes us "Almagri" and that is what makes them Oleva. God knows we have tried to live upto that ideal. Whom do people trust when they need justice? Are the common folks happy in Oleva? Do they get justice? Why do you think most who can leave Oleva and come here, have done so? If we behave like the brute that he is there will be no difference between the two of us'.

'There are some things we will do to keep us and our citizens safe' he continued 'but there are some things we will never do as long as there is another alternative.'

Toshin and Dhyum were both silent as well, contemplating the legend they had just heard from Priyu.

'All this talking has made me thirsty' smiled Priyu.

'And all this listening has made me hungry' laughed out Toshin calling for the house maid to serve dinner.

Over a simple but delicious meal they discussed in detail the plan they had in mind and this time it was Toshin and Dhyum who took the mantle and Priyu listened attentively as they outlaid the sketch and various possible scenarios that could play out and their contingency plan of action.

'We've heard that the village of Sarpatta near the Sarpatta forest and mountain has been troubled the past few days by a wild beast that has turned man-eater. The villagers have been so traumatized that the villagers now strongly believe that it's not a tiger but a demon in the shape of the tiger that has been terrorizing them. The King's guards have also not been able to hunt it so the villagers have got together and have put together a reward for anyone who can kill the beast. I think it will be a good cover for us to go there as hunters for the reward and enter the forest also.'

Priyu looked concerned, 'Could it be true, could it be some possessed spirit?'

'I do not believe in this spirit nonsense' Toshin spoke. 'A tiger or any wild animal for that matter will always try and avoid us. They are forced to hunt humans when there is not enough game in the forest or when the beast is injured or old. We know that the Sarpatta forest has enough gaurs, nilgiris and boars so it cannot be that it is lack of game that has forced it to be a man-eater. It has turned man-eater probably because it is injured or because it has grown old'.

Priyu looked at Dhyum who was thoughtful and quiet. 'What do you think Dhyum?' he asked.

'What Toshin says is true, but we will know soon enough' was his response. 'You don't have to be worried about us. We understand the need of this mission and we may have to do some unpleasant tasks but it has to be done' he added quietly.

Priyu nodded gravely. They discussed a few more details as to the route they will take to reach Oleva, the way they will communicate.

'I believe you have already met with Sanigya in the morning? Did she have something special for you?' Priyu asked.

'Yes' they said in unison. Toshin could not help laughing out loud and even the usually stoic Dhyum broke out in a smile to the puzzlement of Priyu.

7. The Chariot Lady
– Sanigya

7

The Chariot Lady – Sanigya

Sanigya, the old lady famously known as the 'Chariot lady' had called them to her work area in the main factory workshop where the 'Ashwangya' chariot designed by her was built and assembled.

She was a revered old woman who had learnt the trade from her father and who in turn had learnt it from his. She had expanded her skills of designing armaments to engineering and designing a new saddle for the horses that was much more comfortable to both man and beast and it was designed in such a way that horseback riders could also use their bow and arrow while galloping and it had slots built in to carry their swords and spears within easy reach.

She had also developed a 4 horse drawn chariot that would carry upto 6 people for longer durations. She had promised the King that this would revolutionise travel and trade and had been proved right. Her chariots had proved so popular within and outside the Kingdom that they had set up 3 more workshops to build the 'Ashwangya' named after her.

Toshin & Dhyum were greeted by the strong odour of a dozen different types of Oils, dyes, inks, dried leather and the mayhem of a hundred voice and noise of work in progress as they walked in. Toshin immediately perked up as he walked into the workshop surrounded by the energy and chatter of the work smiths and carpenters.

Her 'office' was one long heavily built rectangular table with a few chairs on a raised platform on one end of the vast room. There was a large window to accommodate the morning light and fresh breeze. There was a fine net fixed on the window to keep the insects and dust out. There were no ornamental artifacts or finery of any kind in her office. The only items of decor were small scale models of many different chariots, trolleys and a myriad of other equipment like ladders, saddles and also some construction equipment's like scaffolding, cranes etc were placed on a large wall behind them. Her table itself was cluttered with an array of different items. Strewn across the table were writing material, curious looking weighing and measuring instruments made out of various metals, wood and glass.

From her office they could get a vantage view of the busy workshop a few steps below them. The factory floor was busy with carpenters working on the assembling of the chariots, upholstery work was carried out in another section.

The blacksmiths and foundry work was carried out in another building a little away from the finishing works factory. The foundry had a large chimney which bellowed out thick dark smoke.

No one gave them much heed as Toshin and Dhyum took in the sight of the workshop below and walked around her work area intrigued by the various objects on the wall and on her table. Toshin picked up a curious looking instrument made of copper, it had a complex pattern of thick glass that magnified images and also threw out a prism of colours. Toshin marveled at the rainbow formed when held against the light, when he felt a sharp rap on his wrist.

He turned to see the white haired chariot woman standing with one hand on her hip and the other hand stretched out to take back instrument from Toshin.

'Look what you have done' she scolded Toshin pointing towards her table.

'What have I done?' asked Toshin looking at the cluttered table.

She pointed at her table again and Toshin peered closely at the mayhem of objects on her table and looked back at her enquiringly.

'See that? I wont be able to find my things now. I don't know why people have to come and disrupt my things?' she mumbled as she sifted through the array of objects looking for something.

She was a busy little petite woman, stick thin all dressed in white. She moved busily among the mess on her table and grabbed a thin long wire like stick.

'There you are' she triumphantly declared, raising the thin metal stick in the air like a wand.

Toshin and Dhyum exchanged glances as she pulled one end of the wand in her hand and it grew longer and she pointed it towards Toshin the tip of the long stick almost touching his nose.

'You are a mischievous one' she announced with her eyes narrowed and browed furrows.

'Am I?' Toshin pondered striking an innocent look.

'Quiet' the old lady scolded him again and looked at Dhyum studying him carefully. After a moment of scrutiny she abruptly turned and walked towards the steps that led down to the factory floor.

'Come with me' she said as she strode

Toshin and Dhyum were taken aback by the speed of old lady's stride and had to hurry up to catch up with the dashing figure in white.

They passed by the workshop and exited the building and she rapidly walked to another large room in front of the factory. This looked like a store room where endless rows of parts in metal, tools and fabric was stored. They walked past a row of shelves and reached a door on which she knocked rapidly. A face appeared at a small opening and peered at them from behind the door, he opened the door as soon as he saw the impatient face of the chariot woman who was waving the stick at him.

'come on, come on' she muttered impatiently as the guard undid the bolts from within and opened the door for them to enter.

Toshin half expected her to poke the guard with her stick as they entered the room. They climbed up a very wide flight of stairs hurrying to catch up with her as she flew up the stairs. They walked into an open courtyard where there were a few young men and women who were waiting for them behind a long table. But unlike her own table which was cluttered and messy this table had a few objects neatly arranged and covered with a white cloth.

The group behind the desk stopped their talking and murmuring and stood still looking expectantly and in open admiration as she walked towards the table humming and nodding at the objects on the table.

She stopped at a covered object and tapped at it with her stick.

The young man behind the table quickly uncovered the cloth to reveal the most unique bow they had ever seen. Toshin eyes opened up in amazement as he moved towards the weapon.

Toshin was stopped on his tracks by the stick that was poked at his chest. She shook her head as she pushed him back with the pointed end of the stick and then the stick was pointed towards Dhyum motioning him forward.

Dhyum stepped up to the Bow and studied it before picking it up. The shape of the frame of the bow was made up in three parts instead of the regular single frame. The lower limb and the upper limb were connected at the arrow grip in the centre by bolts. The bow was not made of wood as most bows were made instead it was made of a metal he had only heard of and never seen or felt it as yet.

He picked it up and was surprised at the lightness of the bow inspite of the elaborate design and the bolts and levers on the bow frame. There were 2 strings instead of the single string on the standard bows. He turned a knob at the joint of the grip and the limbs started extending outward enlarging the frame, when he turned it in the other direction the frame shrank making it smaller. The other levers and bolts changed the shape of the bow to different proportions to meet the size of the person of the wielding it and also for the purpose for which it was being used.

She looked on silently as Dhyum tried the various configurations of the bow, testing the strings for the right tension and when he was satisfied she tapped at an arrow kept on the table. She then pointed towards the other end of the courtyard where a fully armoured dummy was placed.

Dhyum picked up the arrow and studied it, the metal head had a dull glow. He placed it on the slot and pulled back the string softly, the frame bent with a smooth arc as he sighted the target through the bow sight. There was a stillness and silence from the expectant crowd as they watched in rapt undivided attention. Dhyum felt the tension in the pull had reached optimum level. There was a zap and a twack as Dhyum let go of the string and the arrow flew out of the bow as fast as lightening as there was a collective sigh of breath being released by the onlookers.

The arrow pierced the armour, shattering the left section of the dummy. There was a ripple of excitement and approval and all walked to the armour to survey the damage.

Toshin picked up the broken piece of the armour to study it. It was made of the standard alloy Almagri soldiers had been using. The arrow had sliced through it cleanly and had lodged in a thick wall made of cork that was placed behind the dummy. Dhyum pulled out the arrow and showed it to Toshin, other than a few scratches on the head and a slight bend on the tip the arrow looked good. The chariot woman picked up the arrow and walked back to the table studying it.

She turned around and narrowed her eyes at Toshin again 'hmm' she murmured to a bemused Toshin. With her stick she pointed at him and he stepped forward smiling to the table. She then pointed at a young woman to unveil another object that was covered by a black cloth. There was a puzzled look on Toshin's face when the young woman uncovered the cloth. Toshin who was expecting another exotic weapon instead found a strange looking object with straps on it. He picked it up curiously it was very light.

'What is it?' he asked the Chariot Lady who was watching him intently.

The young woman who had unwrapped the object moved behind him and strapped it on to him.

'Oh, This is an armour. Very clever it is so light I can hardly feel it' said Toshin moving about. He lifted his hands and remarked 'But I cannot move as well in it'.

The young woman stepped forward and showed him how to adjust the straps and it fit him snuggly.

Toshin moved about the placed flaying his arms, squatting and rolled over and found the armour easy to handle 'It is like it is not on my body at all' he said moving around the place to the amusement of the young men and women watching the two young warriors trying their wares.

'Are you done now?' said the Chariot lady looking a little impatient with Toshin.

'Just one more thing' said Toshin as he took a few steps back and ran towards them summersaulted neatly and came to a stop right in front of the Chariot lady.

Dhyum looked at his friend trying to signal him a but Toshin was enjoying his own show.

'My dear lady' he said clearly for all to hear 'It's a fine piece of garment, I can ride in it, fight wearing it maybe even dance wearing it' he said to the giggles of the young women around them 'But' he said and paused for dramatic affect 'But…the question in my mind is, will it stop an arrow?'

The lady looked at him thoughtfully with hands on her hips.

Toshin looked pleased with himself and started unstrapping himself. The stick which the lady was holding was suddenly whipped and it coiled around Toshin's hand like a spring.

'Oh, it can do that too?' wondered Toshin aloud still smiling.

The lady started walking towards the far end of the courtyard pulling Toshin behind her.

He let himself being led towards the shattered dummy getting alarmed at every step.

'Surely you don't mean to…'

'This is not required'

'My lady…'

All his protests were ignored by the marching lady as she strode towards the dummy and made Toshin stand there in place of the dummy and started walking back towards the table on the other end of the courtyard.

'My dear lady' an alarmed Toshin called out '…I trust you ofcourse, I don't need to know….there are other ways you know…are you listening to me?' shouted a jittery Toshin to the retreating back of the Chariot lady who strode over and handed the bow to a hesitant Dhyum.

When she saw Dhyum hesitate she prodded him with the stick 'come on, come on' she ordered pointing to the right side of his chest, indicating where the arrow should be fired.

Dhyum stood still contemplating when the lady called the guard standing by the door to take Dhyum's place.

Dhyum raised the bow and took aim, the lady walked over to Dhyum and made a few changes to the bolts and immediately Dhyum felt the tension loosen in the strings. She held her stick in front of Dhyum and then raised it and Dhyum released the arrow from the bow.

He saw the arrow hit Toshin and he saw him spin to his right with the force of the impact and collapse to the ground. He was the first one to reach him as the other too raced towards the prone figure of Toshin lying on the far end of the courtyard.

Dhyum reached him and picked him up gently and checked the right breast plate, it was intact. Only Dhyum had realised that the old lady had switched the arrow from the pointed arrow to a dull edged arrow at the very last moment.

Toshin slowly opened his eyes and looked around at all the concerned faces peering at him, the old lady was studying him intently eyes narrowed.

'The old lady is crazy, let us get away from here before she kills me' whispered Toshin.

The lady knelt down and checked his pulse she nodded and Dhyum helped him to his feet.

She called to one of her assistants and conferred with them. The young assistant walked over to Dhyum and a concerned Toshin and said 'Our lady will be leaving us now, but there are a few more items that we have to show you. We will do it over there' she said indicating to a room towards the far end of the courtyard.

Dhyum and a relieved Toshin walked over to the lady to bid her farewell and to take her blessings. She blessed them and as the young warriors turned to follow the assistants Toshin felt a sharp rap on his behind from the Chariot Lady's stick. A surprised and flustered Toshin turned around to look at the old lady saying 'Be careful' and walk away in her customary stride. Toshin & Dhyum thought they heard her chuckle as she walked away.

'So I assume it went well with the Chariot lady' Priyu summarized as he got up to bid them good fortune. 'There is just one more thing to do now, take this' said Priyu handing them a half broken piece of a conch shell. 'Take this with you and give it to my man in Oleva, he will know you are sent by me. He will take care of all your needs.'

It was a worried and sad Priyu that bid his two brave young men goodbye and made his way back to the city of Almagri to await word on the progress and outcome of their mission.

8. The Journey – The Ajoori

8

The Journey – The Ajoori

It was the 3rd day of their journey. Dhyum & Toshin had taken up a detour and had moved south instead of travelling east towards Oleva. They would climb over the mountain range of Vijnya and Bindu and approach the Kingdom of Oleva from the south instead of directly from the Kingdom of Almagri. As their final destination was the Sarpatta forest, it would save them a day of travel and also avoid interrogation and suspicion if they came into the Oleva kingdom directly from the territory of Almagri.

They had travelled steadily with very few stops for the horses to drink and rest. In times of steep climbs they had disembarked and walked along their steads to save their horses energy. The hawk circled above keeping an eye out and calling out if it spotted any prey or predator and Doree the mountain wolf kept his eye open when they took short naps.

They had stopped at the most dominant tribe of the Bindu mountain clan - the Ajoori's, who were much feared and mostly avoided for their unpredictable quick temper and violent ways. The Ajoori's lived in the densest part of the forest frequented by the stripped tiger, sloth bears, king cobras and the wild boars. The Ajoori's had made their living capturing and killing the king of the jungle the biggest cat of them all, the stripped Tiger. They would capture these great beasts and supply them to willing buyers of its skin, teeth, nail and other parts. The cubs of these magnificent cats had a great many buyers too.

As they neared the Ajoori territory Toshin & Dhyum dismounted and walked ahead letting their steads follow them behind with Doree. They had left most of their weapons on their mounts and only carried the bare minimum with them.

Once they had entered the Ajoori territory, they knew that they would be under the watchful eye of the Ajoori. They were sure that the Ajoori's have seen them and are following their every move. The Ajoori's were masters at camouflage and even the falcon above with its keen eyesight would find it difficult to spot them. Dhyum had tied a small purse of coins on the end of his spear which made a jingling sound when they moved. This would warn the Ajoori's as well as any beasts to announce their presence.

They were met by the Ajoori's and taken to their closely guarded settlement. The Ajoori's gave them a resting place and food for the journey ahead in exchange for two exquisite daggers forged by the finest craftsmen of Almagri.

With the permission of the Ajoori's, Toshin & Dhyum had changed their customary Almagri clothes to the attire of the Ajoori tribesman. They applied a mixture of Sandalwood and Neem paste on their bodies which was primarily applied by the Ajoori's to give them cover when they hunted in the Bindu forest by concealing the natural human body odour, they also cut their hair short to match the tribesmen hair and lined their eyes with khol. Though bigger than the average Bindu tribesman they both passed off as them especially since they also spoke some of the Ajoori dialect.

After a much needed night of rest for them and for their animals, the Ajoori guide had safely guided them to the edge of their forest domain avoiding the animal traps laid by them and also from trespassing into enemy territory. They had estimated that they would hit upon the road that led to the southern border of the Oleva Kingdom by sunset and from then on it would take them a day's journey to reach the Oleva Kingdom.

It was nearing sunset when Dhyum held out his fist suddenly to Toshin to stop. They had to now thread carefully ahead as it was Oleva territory. His hawk had returned back to her nest and they would have to rely on their senses for any unseen foe from now on.

They dismounted and left their steads and ventured down slowly on foot, swords drawn. They could hear a small waterfall nearby that would fall on the road ahead and would continue its downward trajectory. It was more like of a stream of water flowing downwards than a waterfall. The small pool of the water created by the stream was a resting place for travelers who quenched their thirst as well as the thirst of their beasts of burden that carried them and their cargo be it bullocks, horse, mule or even elephants. Travelers could even spend the night or cook their meals in a make shift shelter made nearby.

As they crept forward they heard voices and when they parted the leaves blocking their view they saw a group of uniformed men collected near the watering hole. They seemed to be arguing about something. It was a group of around 12 soldiers who looked like Oleva soldiers and they were arguing and trying to reason with a group of people who were hidden from view at the moment. Toshin nudged Dhyum and pointed to the road ahead.

The road leading to the Oleva southern border had caved in leaving a huge gaping hole on their path. That meant that it would be impossible for the soldiers and their fellow travelers to take the mountain path. Toshin also pointed out to an Ox that had a fire torch tied to its horn.

They understood the situation that was playing in front of them.

The unsteady mountain cut path have collapsed due to a landslide. The only option now in front of them was to go back and walk around the mountain which would add another 6 days more to their journey or walk through the dreaded cave tunnel of the Serpent spirit Manusa.

This part of the jungle was believed to be governed by the demi goddess of serpents 'Manusa'. It was believed that the cave ahead was her abode in which she guarded a treasure that was more precious than all the treasures of the world.

The travelers who passed through this part of the mountain offered a sacrifice to the goddess before embarking on their journey further. The sacrifice was in the form of a goat or a cow usually led to the entrance of the cave. There was a boulder that covered the entrance. A fire torch would be tied to the animal and it would be led to the entrance of the cave and pushed inside and the boulder would be placed back to cover the entrance of the cave. It was also understood that the cave was actually a tunnel and had an exit on the other end, as on one occasion the sacrificial animal was found further down the mountain path.

But no one dared to actually enter the cave. The fable of the treasure had tempted a few brave adventurers who had ventured into the cave in search of this hidden treasure but were never seen again.

Toshin and Dhyum looked at each other and there was an unspoken communication between the two. They put their swords back, gathered their steads and announced their presence to the Oleva soldiers by noisily walking towards the water pool. The soldiers stopped their chatter and were at once on alert watching the two tall Ajoori tribesman walk up towards them rather briskly.

Anyone who knew about the Ajoori's were wise enough to be on guard when the Ajoori's were around. They also knew that it was best not to provoke or confront the proud and often reckless Ajoori who considered it their honour to die a brave death in battle or a hunt rather than die of old age or sickness.

The soldiers parted quietly making way for the two Ajoori's and their horses towards the water pool. Toshin and Dhyum like true Ajoori's ignored the soldiers and walked past them and drank their fill from the pool and allowed their horses and Doree to drink as well as the rest of the crowd looked on.

The captain of the Soldier counted the no of piercing on their nose and ears to estimate the hierarchy of the two Ajoori's and imagined that they must be quite high up and seasoned hunter warriors from the no of piercings on their ears.

Dhyum & Toshin observed discreetly that the group of people the soldiers were having a heated argument were what looked like a group of monks of some order. They were not familiar with this order. This group numbered six of them backed against the entrance of the sacred cave that was called the abode of the Serpent spirit Manusa.

Toshin & Dhyum quickly understood that the root of the dispute between the soldiers and the people from this group was the route to be taken. The monks wanted to turn back and go around the mountain and the soldiers wanted to pass through the dreaded Manusa tunnel.

They also guessed that the monks were somehow important to the Oleva cause as the soldiers were arguing and trying to reason with them instead of forcibly moving them as soldiers were accustomed to do. Toshin and Dhyum wondered as to what was the urgency of the soldiers that they were ready to brave the dangers of the tunnel than walk around the mountain.

The arrival of Toshin & Dhyum had put a temporary halt to their haggling as the soldiers were now focused on the Ajoori tribesmen in their midst. The Ajoori's were an autonomous mountain tribe who did not recognize any Kingdom and owed their allegiance to no King outside their own Tribal chief. There was an uneasy truce between the Ajoori's and the surrounding Kingdoms and they were mostly left alone as they were a small tribe minding their own business and preferred to stay within their own mountain fiefdom. They had no ambition to grow and capture other lands and there was an unwritten understanding with the Olevas that their mountains will not be targeted and only used as a route to traverse.

The captain of the Oleva squad approached them cautiously yet trying to maintain an image of command 'Which way are you two headed?' he asked with what he expected to be an authoritative voice but fell far short of his expectations.

The two warriors looked up from their relaxed resting position and Toshin the more aggressive of the two spat out 'What is it to you?' while Dhyum looked on unperturbed.

The captain was flustered by the brusque put off and was fumbling for words when Dhyum put him out of his misery by saying 'Sarpatta' nonchalantly.

'hmm' the Captain considered this. He wisely chose to refrain from enquiring further and walked back to his soldiers and conferred with them.

'They are going to Sarpatta' he told his soldiers who had gathered around him.

'Why do you think?' his deputy asked him

'Why don't you ask them?' his Captain asked him irritated.

'Who is going to Sarpatta?' the question was asked by one of the monks of the order who had overheard the soldiers talking.

The captain turned to the monk who had asked the question. She was a middle aged woman in the plain grey robe of the order. She like all the other monks of her order had their heads tonsured and wore no finery, jewels or flowers of any kind. There was no kohl in her eyes, no scent of the jasmine on their body or the comfort of a footwear. They were all barefoot and seemed to have no possession save a small satchel slung over their shoulders.

'They are going to Sarpatta' the captain spoke to the woman indicating the Ajoori with his chin.

'Do you know why they are going there?' she enquired in her steady voice. She spoke with the clarity and clearness of one who has learnt to focus their thoughts and energy. She maintained steady eye contact when she spoke and her voice never wavered.

The captain was a little uncomfortable with this woman who seemed to look into his soul when she looked at him.

'No' he answered slowly.

She turned and walked towards the Ajoori's before the Captain could act.

'I understand that you both are going to Sarpatta?' she asked them standing right next to the two resting Ajoori's.

Toshin and Dhyum opened their eyes and regarding this woman standing in front of them in bare feet and a steady gaze.

'So?' was Toshin's response.

'Why are you going there?' she persisted calmly.

'Who is asking this question?' he asked lazily lying on the ground next to Dhyum who had his eyes on the woman.

'I am from Sarpatta' she said flatly.

The two stole quick glances at each other 'For the 20 cattle head reward' was the nonchalant response from Toshin, but they were both observing her with interest.

She remained calm regarding them silently. There was silence and stillness. She was standing straight, her gaze direct and deep, her hands lightly resting on each other. She could have been mistaken for a statue carved out of grey stone. The Ajoori's themselves known for their patience and stillness remained still in their sitting position, easily and serenely.

'I wish you good fortune' she said to them quietly and walked away before they could respond to talk to the Captain and the other monks of her order.

'What did they say to you?' asked the captain as the woman joined them.

'They will guide us through this….' she said pointing to the cave opening. She spoke clearly for her voice to be heard by Toshin and Dhyum who once again exchanged glances without saying anything.

'What? did they really say that?' asked a puzzled captain.

He felt relief but he could also feel the discomfort of the soldiers with the idea of the unpredictable Ajoori's in their midst. On the other hand the Ajoori's knew the jungle well and it would be handy to have two skilled hunter warriors on their side if they were to be attacked by man or beast and especially to cross the dreaded tunnel that lay in front of them.

'But what do they want in return?' asked the bewildered captain.

'5 pieces of gold' she replied.

'5?' he said astonished, 'What would the Ajoori do with that kind of money?'

'Why don't you ask them?' she said as she moved to her order who were all waiting for her and conferred with them.

The Captain was undecided with the idea and turned to speak to his deputy.

Meanwhile the Toshin and Dhyum stood up making preparations to continue their journey.

She looked at the captain patiently, a hint of a smile playing on her clear smooth features 'Captain you better make your mind fast, if you want to save an Ox' she said looking at the Ox with the torch tied to its horns. 'And' she added 'To save yourselves' she spoke with authority for all the other soldiers to hear. There was a murmur within the soldiers as they considered their options of having someone like the fearless and fearsome Ajoori being a part of their travel.

The captain walked over to the Ajoori's and addressed them 'come with us' he once again failed to sound convincing.

The Ajoori's stopped what they were doing and turned slowly to the captain 'we didn't hear that' said Toshin bending his ear towards him. Small beads of sweat began to form on the captain's forehead inspite of the evening chill.

'…er what I mean is, I welcome you to join us' he managed to very softly '….please?' he added in a whisper, praying that his men were out of earshot.

Toshin and Dhyum exchanged knowing glances.

The monk had joined them at this point 'Just give them the money' she told him firmly.

Toshin and Dhyum were surprised when they heard talk of money from the monk but didn't react and turned to secure their mounts.

'Ok' the uncomfortable Captain said, glad that this negotiation was over. 'I will give them the money but they take the first lead in the tunnel'.

'Bring me the torch's' she commanded a soldier who was holding on to the Ox. Who did so as he was told.

She took the torch's from the soldier and handed them a torch each and said 'Come with us to Oleva.'

9. The Journey – The Manusa Cave Of Terror

9

The Journey – The Manusa Cave Of Terror

Toshin & Dhyum took some time to adjust to the lack of light inside the tunnel. The only source of light were the two torches held by them. They had left Doree to stay with their steads. They did not have the exquisite Bow and arrow which Sanigya the Chariot woman had made for them. An Ajoori tribesman would look out of place with such an exquisite weapon and surely that would attract unwanted attention, so Dhyum and Toshin carried a ordinary bow similar to what the Ajoori's used but they were surely glad for the lightweight armour they were wearing underneathh their attire.

Before they had started they had collected some smooth round edged white stones, they would drop them at intervals for the rest to follow later.

The tunnel had quickly narrowed down to a narrow descent. They imagined their horses might just squeeze in single file but they would worry about that later. The cave was tall enough and the walls were damp and wet from the seepage of water. The constant moisture had made the walls slippery with green algae and moss on it. They could also see calcite formations that hung from the ceiling of the cave above. They could hear the drip of water ahead suggesting that they are near a pool of water somewhere.

They moved cautiously ahead, relying on their sense of hearing and smell as much as their sight. They strained their eyes and ears for the slightest movement and sound and took each step with caution.

They continued a little further when Toshin whispered to Dhyum 'Can you smell that?' There was a pungent smell that seemed to burn their nostrils ever so slightly.

Dhyum nodded and removed a twig from his belt pocket and broke it into two and handed one piece to Toshin. They both inhaled deeply from the twig Dhyum had provided and they crushed it in their hands and applied the crushed powder on their nose and nostrils and felt the burning sensation subside but they were feeling a sensation of giddiness and lightheadedness as they came to a bend in the cave, ahead it was pitch dark.

Toshin reached for his belt and removed a palm sized flat stone that shone in the reflected light. He placed the stone in front of the fire torch and it amplified the light and threw a beam of light at least 20 steps ahead. They could now see two paths ahead of them, both dark and both quiet, one taking them to the left and the other leading to the right. Toshin placed his torch in both the entrances. In the second cave the flame of his torch started flickering much more than the first one. They decided to take that direction and Toshin dropped one of the white stones on the entrance of the right side cave as they entered it. Toshin put back the light reflecting stone in his belt as they did not want whatever spirit or beast that was there to know of their presence.

As they moved into the second cave the burning toxic stench grew stronger. They wet a piece of cloth and tied it around their nose and they moved ahead. Dhyum stopped and pointed to Toshin, he had to strain his eyes to see a faint red glow in the distance. They stood still trying to listen, they would hear something like squeals, it was a high pitched distant squeal. They moved cautiously towards the red glow, which was now getting stronger and stronger and so was the stench. The path had widened enough for them to walk side by side. The walls had curved like the shape of a large boat with a narrow bottom and widening curved walls.

Dhyum suddenly raised his fist and his dagger flew into his hands 'Quick the light' he said.

Toshin had also heard the sudden rustling and slithering sound. Something was coming towards them from the dark at a frantic pace.

Toshin quickly placed the stone in front of the torch and pointed the beam towards the sound. It was the largest snake that they had ever seen. They could only see the large head and the angry eyes and had no idea where it ended. Its trunk was as thick as a bamboo tree and it was slithering fast towards them. There was no time for the bow, Dhyum quickly pointed to a ledge above them on eighter side of the wall and he managed to scamper up the slippery side wall of the cave, Toshin had done likewise on the opposite side of the wall. He had immediately removed the reflecting stone and put it away.

In their hurry to climb up they barely had time to look down when to their horror they realized that the snake was not running towards them but it was running away from something.

They watched mystified and in growing horror as the head of the snake passed them without looking at them and as the long body of the snake passed beneath them they heard the squealing and swarm of a thousand rats chasing the snake, some had already clambered up the long body of the snake biting into it and taking chunks of the snake with their ferocious bites. These rats were nothing like the house mouse and gutter rats they had come across. They were the size of a small cat with hard pointy fur and the blood red beady eyes that cast a red glow in the otherwise dark tunnel.

Dhyum looked at Toshin concerned, from the pale glow of the torch Dhyum could see that the blood had trained from Toshin's face and he was frozen with fear. He could not move and his gaze was fixed on the carnage below as the bloodthirsty rodents climbed upon each other in their haste to reach the dying snake. The squeal of the rats was deafening as they preyed and feasted on their mortal enemy.

Dhyum tried to divert Toshin's attention to him. 'Psst' he whispered as softly as he could.

Toshin tore his eye away from the rats below and closed his eyes. Tears had formed in his eyes and he was trembling. He steadied himself and slowly opened his eyes to see the focused anxious look of Dhyum. He held his gaze as Dhyum shook his head as if to say 'Not here, not this way, NO!'

Toshin exhaled and nodded to Dhyum, he wiped his sweaty palms against his clothes and even managed a weak smile to communicate that he was okay.

They slowly started looking for ways out of there without making a noice as they did not want to attract the attention of the hungry rats below. When all of a sudden there was complete silence. All the rats had stopped what they were doing and had stopped devouring the snake. They slowly parted and made way as Toshin and Dhyum saw a black mass of pointy hair slowly made its way through the mass of rats. They could not believe the rize of the King rat as it made its way to the half dead snake, it was the size of a small boar and its snorted just like one. The claws scratched against the cave floor and made a grating noise as it walked past the cowering rats and trampled and crunched and spit out any rat that was not fast enough to get out of its path.

The mortally wounded snake lay panting as the King rat approached it slowly. The snake tried to wiggle and turn around to get into a better position but the rat quickly sprung and catch the enormous snake just below its head and sunk its teeth into the huge withering serpent as it shook so hard that the rats that were latched on it body were flung around. The blood soaked reptile and the rodent engaged in a bloody battle as the rest of the rats too joined in the melee.

Toshin pointed to cave wall above Dhyum which had another ridge. It would only be a matter of time before the rats devoured the reptile and look for their next victim. Dhyum climbed up carefully towards the ridge which seemed like a narrow passage and had enough room for him to stand almost straight. Toshin also slowly started climbing up and was able to cross over carefully to the side where Dhyum was. Toshin was able to breathe normally once he was standing next to Dhym. They saw that they were at least away from the rats for the moment, but they still had to find a way out without being spotted.

They walked along this narrow ridge in the opposite direction to the snake and mayhem below. They reached a small opening in the ridge, it was another small cave on the wall of the ridge and they both hesitated at the mouth of the small entrance. Toshin pointed to the floor of the cave, it was smooth and soft, unlike the rest of the cave which was rough and hard. This cave had smooth soft soil on it and there was not a damp spot on the walls or the floor. Toshin slowly removed the reflecting stone and shone the torch light in this little cave. The torch filled the small cave chamber with light and what they saw in the corner froze their blood. There in the far corner was what looked like the female version of the King rat they had seen below. This large rodent had laid down and at least 10 small hairless rodent attached to it teats drinking from it. They had walked into the nest of the largest blood thirsty rodent they had ever seen and now it was looking directly at them and it did not look pleased at all.

The Queen rodent got up slowly and shook its litter free from her teats. Dhyum & Toshin removed their short swords and readied themselves for the attack. As Toshin moved the beam of his torch fell on the young rats and they screeched and squealed into a corner behind their mother. Toshin realized that the rodents in this cave were not used to light and shone his light on the eyes of the large queen rodent which maddened her further as she screeched and screamed.

'Now' cried Toshin as Dhyum flew across and tried to sink his dagger into the squirming rodent but just as Dhyum crossed the beam it got blocked for a brief moment which was enough for the rodent to spring quickly to its side. It moved very quick inspite of its bulk and Dhyum missed the neck and instead struck its back which was a solid mass of muscle and instead of piercing flesh it merely grazed the skin making a cut.

It was now on the other side of the cave circling them like a tiger contemplating its next move, Toshin tried to blind it with the beam but it kept shaking it head avoiding the beam. Its litter had moved with it behind her but one of the young one was left behind, Toshin quickly kicked it and this made the queen rat look at Toshin and he found the perfect time to shine the light into its beady red eyes, as it screamed in pain Dhyum shot across and buried his sword with all his might in the neck of the big rodent. It gave out the most ear piercing screech as it collapsed on the floor of the cave.

'Quick' said Dhyum has they moved out of the cave.

In the process Dhyum's torch had been extinguished and Toshin's torch was now low, they reached the mouth of the cave nest and outside on the ledge just a few steps away from them they faced a thousand red beady eyes. There was one eye bigger than the rest and it snorted so loud that the fine dust from the floor of the ledge blew up.

'Quick the flint stone' Dhyum said to Toshin who fumbled in his belt pocket for the flint and struck it against the wall of the cave and there was a long bright spark as Dhyum quickly relit his extinguished torch. The march of the rat colony was temporarily stopped as they were confronted by the beam of light from the fire torch of Dhyum and Toshin as they surveyed each other on the narrow ledge. Down below them the tail end of the carcass of the great snake lay stripped to the bone.

'Quick do it again' said Dhyum

There was no response from Toshin

'Toshin' shouted Dhyum and Toshin was shook out of his stupor.

'Do what?'

'Rub the flint against the wall…quick' he shouted.

Toshin rubbed the flint stone against the wall and there was the spark again and this time it was longer and there was a small flame which died down slowly.

'See that?' said Dhyum hurriedly 'There is something in this liquid that is catching fire'.

Toshin had barely time to answer when the Queen rodent gave out one last dying squeal and the huge angry black mass of the King rat launched at them with the fury and anger of a wounded beast.

'Jump' shouted Dhyum as they both jumped from the ledge to the cave floor below. They landed on the carcass of the dead snake and looked up as the King rat looked down upon them and leaped directly at Toshin.

Toshin swiped at the large leaping rodent with his sword but missed it as the rodent landed on Toshin. Toshin fell to the floor under the weight of the rodent on top of him. They rolled on the floor battling as Dhyum struck at its hind legs with all his might. It gave a scream of hurt and anger and released its hold on Toshin's neck as it turned slowly towards Dhyum. The rest of the rodents had jumped down and stayed one step behind the King rodent inching their way slowly towards the two warriors.

'Are you hurt?' cried a concerned Dhyum.

'Yes, a little but I am fine' gasped Toshin as he struggled to his feet.

They kept waving their fire torch to the advancing rodents to keep them at bay but they knew they could not hold them back for long as they were getting bolder and bolder. The King rat was cut badly on its hind leg by Dhyum's strike and Toshin's dagger was lodged in it shoulder but it did not seemed to notice the dagger sticking out it only looked angrier as it dragged its leg but still continued marching towards the duo.

They slowly backed up the narrow cave when Toshin felt the damp trickle of liquid on the damp wall of the cave. He instinctively placed his torch near the water trickle and it quickly caught fire sending a red flame of fire up the wall.

'Do this' Dhyum shouted, placing his torch near the damp wall which immediately shot out a fire ball up the wall. Toshin followed suit and lit his side of the wall, this stopped the rodents on their tracks long enough for the duo to turn their backs and run down the cave.

They only had a moments head start when they glanced back they saw that the fire had died down and now the swarming wave of red beady eyes were coming at them like a giant red angry tsunami.

'This way' shouted Dhyum as they raced down the cave slipping and falling. They were following the sound of the dripping liquid as it got louder and louder.

The rats were almost on them as they could see a puddle of smelly liquid in front of them.

'ahhh' screamed Toshin as a couple of rats jumped on him from above, he plucked them out of his neck and threw them in the puddle and lit it as the little puddle caught fire and burned the two rats that were thrown in it.

'Here' screamed Toshin as the narrow cave suddenly opened up into a large chamber. There was a big pool of this contaminated water and the strong odour of oil in this chamber was overwhelming but to Toshin and Dhyum they never loved any other smell better than the strong smell of this liquid as they both jumped into it with their torches extinguished. The liquid was waist high and they quickly waded to the other end with the rats in close pursuit.

Toshin jumped up to the other end quick in a flash wiped out the flint stone.

'Wait' said Dhyum before Toshin could light his torch.

Dhyum quickly removed his clothes as Toshin understood and removed his soaked garments himself. Dhyum lit his soaked cloth and threw it in the midst of the liquid pool and Toshin did likewise. The pool of liquid was now filled with the rats chasing them. The pool burst into a ball of fire as the cave lit up with a waterfall of fire burning up the large brood of rats that had jumped into the pool along with the king rat that screeched and screamed. The few that had made it across were quickly cut down by them.

Toshin and Dhyum did not wait for to watch the spectacle of the burning rodents as they made their way out of the large cave. Thick smoke filled the chamber and they ran in the direction of the wind that was blowing their torch flame and were relieved to see a ray of light filtering in from a thick growth of vegetation. They cut through the foliage and were relieved to came to the other end of the tunnel and collapsed on the floor coughing and panting.

'I thought you were gone' said Dhyum panting 'when I saw that rat on you'

'Even I thought so' said an exhausted Toshin, lying on his back. 'Only this saved me' he said tapping at the neck brace he had worn which the Chariot Woman had made for them. 'I thank that crazy old woman for saving my life' he said panting on the floor.

'I can never be the same around a rat now' shivered Toshin, tending to the scratches and bites on his neck and shoulders.

'Are you okay?' he asked Dhyum. Dhyum nodded.

'Let's give some time for the smoke to clear and then we can signal them to follow' he said.

After a while Dhyum placed a burning arrow on his bow and shot the fire arrow high up in the sky signaling to the rest of their group behind to start their journey through the cave and join them at the other end.

It was a while later the rest of the travel party joined them at the other end of the tunnel, they had followed the white pebbles left behind by Toshin and Dhyum. Doree rushed to them and showed his happiness by rubbing against them.

'I missed you too, we are fine' Dhyum said softly to Doree patting her back and scratching her ears.

The woman in grey walked up to them with the Captain of the Oleva's. She inspected them both and walked back to her group.

'I saw the dead snake and the…' the captain mumbled, 'what were they? Rats? I have never seen one like that. A few were alive almost took one of my man down' he said pointing to a soldier who was laid down and tended by the monks of the order.

The woman returned back to them with a bowl of thick paste and wordlessly started applying it to the wounds of Dhyum and Toshin.

The captain turned to go 'uh' he hesitated 'The men and me are grateful to you' he said awkwardly and placed 5 gold coins in Dhyum's palm and walked away quickly to look at the wounds of his men.

'You both are brave' said the woman 'You make your people proud' she said as she applied the paste on their wounds.

10. In Enemy Territory

10

In Enemy Territory

They reached the southern border of the Oleva Kingdom the next morning without any further incident. They were not stopped or questioned at the border as they were part of the contingent that consisted of the Oleva soldiers and the monks of the Austram order.

On the way, Toshin & Dhyum had come to know of the monks a little more. The Austram monks were a highly revered order consisting of women only. They welcomed widows and orphans into their fold or any woman wanting to give up their material life and live a life of celibacy and worship.

Their abode was the Vijnya mountain that was neighboring the Bindu mountain range. They lived an austere self-sufficient life of growing their own food and making their own clothes.

Toshin & Dhyum had come to understand that the monks in grey were very knowledgeable in the medical properties of herbs & roots and they often worked as nurses in the battlefield. They also took care of the terminally sick and the outcasts of society.

Toshin & Dhyum listened to the woman attentively as she spoke to them and told them about their way of living.

Dhyum was especially interested in all of the medicinal gains and knowledge they had acquired from their study and practice. He discussed at length on the medicinal properties of the various herbs, plants and roots they grew and gathered from the forests. He was fascinated to know of the use of a certain algae in nutrition and healing.

They also came to know about the reason for the monks visiting the city. They were called by the King Oleva to perform the 'Austro' a ceremony performed before a battle or expedition to bring good fortune to the Kingdom.

They asked her about Sarpatta and her life there but that was met with silence and they could not elicit more information from her about Sarpatta.

As neared outskirts of the city, Toshin and Dhyum turned to the group to bid them farewell. She walked up to them and to bid them farewell and good luck. She removed a flower from her bag and handed the flower to Toshin.

Toshin studied the flower as he had never seen such a strange flower before.

'What is this flower?' he asked her.

'It is the Sara flower' she answered and added cryptically 'May it help you in what you seek' and left them with the soldiers towards the city.

Toshin turned towards Dhyum and showed him the flower, Dhyum shrugged thoughtfully.

As they moved towards the Kingdom of Oleva they noticed the visible change in environment and the mood of the place. The city around them spoke of past splendour and better times gone by. It seemed like a once prosperous city now living in reminiscence and denial. Crumbling old monuments dotted the streets which needed cleaning and upkeep.

Soon they reached the heart of the city, the marketplace. There was a somber mood about the marketplace. There was none of the gaiety, music, laughter and the colour of Almagri. There were no chatter of children playing around, the giggle of young girls or the gossip and discussion of the elderly at the town square.

The people went about their business in a sullen silence. The merchants and shop keepers of the bazar spoke of tough times and lost trade. Most of the people they met seemed upset and on edge, even a simple request for direction was met with a suspicious and skeptic look. It was high noon when they decided to walk into an eating place and were surprised to find that they had to pay in advance for a meal which was unheard of in Almagri.

They saw columns of soldiers making their way to the outskirts of the city which was once a meeting ground. They saw horses, elephants and chariots been moved towards that direction.

'I do not understand this' said Dhyum to Toshin as they were walking in the main street of Oleva after their meal.

'What don't you understand?'

'This' he answered, moving his arms around. 'Clearly the Kingdom is crumbling and the people need help, so what does the King do? He starts a war, a war he surely cannot afford.'

'Why do you think he is doing it?' he asked rhetorically. 'Does he want to divert attention? Is he greedy or is this an ego driven mad crusade to make a legacy for himself?'

'All of above and most importantly' added Toshin 'he is a total idiot.'

They walked along the street casually till they reached a shop selling beautiful artifacts and statues made of stone, marble and clay. They stopped to admire the handicrafts. One particular life size statue of a woman and child caught the attention of Toshin as he entered the shop to take a closer look at it and called the shopkeeper over to him.

'This is a beautiful piece of art' Toshin complimented him.

'Thank you kind sir' the shopkeeper said 'I am sure it will make your house look beautiful'

'I hope so too. Will it survive salt water?' asked Toshin looking him dead in the eye.

The merchant paused for a while and looked up at Toshin & Dhyum 'How do you propose to pay for this?'

'With this' said Toshin removing the half broken Conch shell which Priyu had given to them when he had bid goodbye.

'Wait here please' said the merchant taking the broken piece of shell with him and went inside his workshop and closed the door behind him. He opened his drawer and unwrapped a piece of broken shell and matched the two half's together. They were a perfect match, they fitted nicely to complete the whole shell.

He came back and told them to follow him inside. They entered an inner room which was a store and a workshop. There were a variety of artifacts, statues and murals in different stages of completion. He walked over to a tall clay idol standing by the corner of the room.

He picked up a hammer and smashed the tall clay idol and opened it. In the hollow of the idol was the shining exquisite Arrow of Sanigya and various other weapons from Almagri.

'A gift from our dear Almagri' he said turning towards them.

The artifact merchant had arranged for them to stay the night there. They were to leave for Sarpatta at sunrise the next day. Before they left the city, they decided to explore the city a little more. They walked towards the outskirts of the city and tried to get as close to the meeting ground where a division of the Oleva army had assembled.

They squatted as the Ajoori's do under a banyan tree some distance away from the encampment.

'Lets head back' Toshin spoke to Dhyum, but something had caught Dhyum's eye.

'What is it?' asked Toshin.

Dhyum pointed to a nondescript house that was a little distance away from the encampment on a hillock.

'Yes, what about it?' asked Toshin looking at the dull grey building that looked like any ordinary dwelling there he had seen in the town.

'Look at it properly' urged Dhyum.

Toshin studied the building attentively as they left the banyan tree and walked casually towards the small structure. On closer inspection it did not look like a house nor any official building. It was a plain structure with no ornamentation or finesse. It was a bare looking small building but it was neat and tidy. As they walked closer Toshin saw it, the tree full of the beautiful Sara flowers that the woman had given them. The house was surrounded by the trees bearing the flower showering the poor looking dwelling with colour and beauty.

They walked up to the structure and entered its front yard.

'Can you smell that?' asked Dhyum.

'Yes, What are we smelling? The smell is very familiar' asked Toshin.

'We are smelling the Sara flower' said Dhyum 'You are finding it familiar because we have been smelling it soon after we exited the Tunnel on the Bindu mountain' he concluded.

'I don't like it when you speak in riddles' said Toshin.

'He is right' said a familiar voice. The woman in grey from the Austrom monk order was standing by the door. She moved to Toshin and removed the bandage on his neck which she had applied to cure the rat bite.

As she removed the bandage, there it was – the familiar smell. The ointment she had applied was made of the Sara flower.

'hmm it is curing well' she said inspecting the wound. 'It's a good thing you both are here, it is time to change your bandages' she said moving inside and they followed her.

'What is this place?' asked Toshin.

'This is where we take care of the wounded and the very sick' she said as they walked along a corridor with rooms to their left and in the center there was an open courtyard. There were other younger women of their order grinding and boiling and cleaning.

They passed them and she stopped at a door. This door was closed and locked from the outside. She took in a deep breath and said 'There is someone in this room, I think you should speak to him.' She hesitated before she added 'But be gentle and don't make any sudden moves'. She steeled herself before she opened the door.

When they entered the room she asked them to stand near the door and she went to a man who was lying on a bed in the room. There was a window next to the bed which was open and that filled the room with the fading light. They looked around to see that the room had candles and lamps in every corner of the room, but they were not lit at the moment.

There was a rough table next to the bed which had some cups and some bottles and the room was filled with the strong sense of incense. The woman sat gently next to the sleeping man. Dhyum and Toshin saw that the man's face was heavily bandaged and they could see only half of his face. The left side of his face including his eye were bandaged.

She caressed his head soothingly and whispered to him. The man opened his eye and they could see a look of relief in the wounded man's eye when he saw the serene face of the woman in front of him. He turned towards the door and that look of relief turned into fear and panic the moment he saw the tall figures of two men in their Ajoori clothes. He tried to say something but words seemed to get stuck in his mouth as he wordlessly flayed his arm at the two strangers in the room.

Toshin & Dhyum stayed still without making any moment and they looked down avoiding eye contact to make themselves less threatening.

'It's all right, it's alright' she spoke to him soothingly 'They are friends, they are here to make things better'.

She held his hand and whispered to him soothingly inviting in Toshin & Dhyum. They advanced towards them slowly showing him their every movement. He watched them like a cornered prey curling up in fear as they stood near the far end of his bed. They saw that he had lost half of his left hand too.

'They want your help' she said to the man who had closed his eyes in the curled fetal position. He did not move and remained in that curled position while the woman sang him a lullaby lovingly stroking his hair. This seemed to calm him a little as he relaxed and slowly straightened himself but he kept his eyes shut and clutched on to the woman tightly.

'Aru…' she whispered to him again 'Aru, these men are good men, they are here to help you. They need your help.'

A look of enquiry and puzzle flash through his face as he opened his eyes and looked at the men standing in front. He looked from them to the woman.

'They are hunters, they are warriors' she said 'They will go to Sarpatta and they will kill the beast'

The moment she said the beast the man started trembling so violently that the woman and Dhyum had to hold him down gently so that he doesn't hurt himself.

'I think we should better leave' he told her and he and Toshin started for the door.

'Don't go' the trembling man cried.

They both stopped and turned to look at him.

'Don't….go…to… Sarpatta…' he trembled violently and his words came out in spasms. 'The village is cursed….it is not a beast…' he struggled to speak.

They both listened carefully as he continued 'It is a not a beast' he said continuously.

'What is it?' asked Toshin.

'It is the demon' he managed to say with a burst of effort. They could see that he was struggling with his fear to talk to them.

'What do you mean?' asked Dhyum.

'It's the black death, with evil eyes. I have never seen such evil eyes...' he cried 'The eyes' he screamed 'The eyes...I see it everywhere...it follows me everywhere' he sobbed uncontrollably.

'What did you see? 'Was it a black leopard?' asked Toshin gently.

The man seemed to reflect on that question 'Yes and No' he said finally.

'What do you mean?'

'It looked like a leopard but it was not moving and behaving like a normal leopard...it was possessed by the demon and...it had green eyes...' he said exhausted with the effort of recounting his horror.

Dhyum and Toshin waited for the woman to join them as they waited for her outside the room when she calmed him and put him to sleep.

She walked with them to the yard. 'He was one of the seven men who were sent by the village to hunt the beast.' She informed them. 'He is the only one that came back. They were strong young men like you are but they were not seasoned hunters. They were desperate villagers fighting to save their livelihood and lives. We have tilled and cultivated the lands near Sarpatta for centuries. That is our home' she paused, her lips trembled ever so slightly as she corrected herself 'Was my home'.

She paused for a while gathering her thoughts and spoke after a heavy sigh 'You still have time…to reconsider' she said. 'You can go back now if you want, but I know and you know that you will not turn back. I wanted you to meet him so that you know what you are about to face there.' she said.

'Is he your only son?' asked Dhyum.

The woman looked up at Dhyum and apart from a solitary tear running down her face, her face was as serene and peaceful as it always was 'No' she said quietly. Only the intake of two quick breaths was any indication that she was fighting her inner struggle 'My elder son was also part of the hunt.'

'I have something for you' she said quickly turning away from them.

She called one of the girls to bring them some of the paste to be applied on their wounds.

'We have something for you too' said Dhyum as they received the paste from the woman.

He clasped a small tightly bound cloth purse in her hand as they left her.

Inside was the 5 gold coins which the Oleva Captain had given them.

11. The Rohini Saga

11

The Rohini Saga

Prince Brihu woke up with a start 'who is there?' he called out. His cabin was dark and quiet, the only thing he heard was the gentle lapping of the waves against the hull of the large yatch.

The door to his cabin was opened urgently by an elderly maid letting in daylight into the otherwise dark room.

'Did you call, your majesty?' she asked walking into his cabin.

'I heard something' he hesitated.

'What was it, your majesty' the old maid asked gently.

'I heard someone whisper….no I heard a hissing' he said.

She walked to a window which was partially open and shut it tight 'It is just the wind son' she said gently sitting next to him.

'Come now son, sleep for a while I will be sitting right here she said' fanning him.

He laid down obediently but his eyes were wide open staring at the ceiling.

'She still comes in my dream' he said looking at the ceiling. 'I can still smell her breath on me, that decaying smell of hers as she......' he shuddered.

'She is a distant memory, she is only a bad dream' the old lady tried to assure him.

'No…no…she has come back. She had promised me, that she would have her vengeance' he said frantically reaching out to his left leg. She watched him in concern as he tried to feel his leg which was no longer there. What was left was a stump above his left knee.

'Hush my child' the old lady spoke soothingly dabbing the sweat from his forehead.

'I will not let that evil witch anywhere near you my son. I promise' she consoled the Prince as he drifted off to a tired sleep.

Priyu stood up and stretched. He was in a large efficient looking room that overlooked the town square. This was one of the offices he used when he was not in the palace office.

He walked over to the window and looked at the street below.

The morning rush had subsided and most of the shops and traders had closed for the afternoon lunch break. In the distance he could see the shore line and the ships docked in the port of Almagri. Even the loading and unloading activity at the port had ceased as the porters were taking a well-deserved break in the shades.

There was a knock at the door and Priyu found a messenger waiting with a sealed envelope. It was the General's seal on the envelope. Inside was a message written in a rough uneven hand, which Priyu recognized as the General's writing. It simply read "Salt and Sand".

Priyu burned the paper and closed and locked the room behind him as he left.

Priyu exited through the back door of his office building alone. He was never comfortable with the idea of travelling with his security guards. Many of the ministers he knew used their guards more to show their clout than for purposes of security and Priyu was not the kind who wanted attention.

He quickly walked through the small alley way that led to the main street and at the mouth of the alleyway he saw an ordinary but sturdy horse drawn carriage waiting for him. Priyu got into the carriage to find the General and Archika waiting for him inside. No greetings were required as the General tapped the roof of the carriage for it to start moving.

Priyu and the others sat in silence as the carriage started moving. He parted the window curtain to see that they were headed towards the shoreline, here the carriage turned away from the port gate and moved parallel to the port. He could see large trader ships docked at the port. Ships that brought in metal, coal, textile and other products and took back finished metal equipment, arms, timber, clothes, fish, coffee and other produce of the land.

A little ahead he saw the large naval boats and he saw some activity as the boats were being readied no doubt in preparation for any eventuality by the General. The General pointed at a handsome yatch docked a little distance away from the naval ships. Priyu and Archika both recognized the royal boat that was the pride of the Prince Brihu.

'Yes? I know whom it belongs to' said Archika looking at the General.

'Look at it closely' suggested the General as both Priyu and Archika peered to get a closer look, then Priyu noticed the smoke coming out of a small chimney on the yatch. He also noticed that there were more guards and horse drawn carriages than usual around the yatch.

'Hmm It is more serious that I had imagined' said Priyu looking towards the yatch.

'Yes' the General answered somberly.

'What is serious?' asked Archika

'That is Prince Brihu's boat' answered Priyu in explanation.

'And that is a cow over there, will you both stop talking in riddles? That is my job' said Archika.

'The Prince has been living here, the last few days. Well since that day and he has not stepped out of the boat the last 2 days' explained the General. 'There is someone I want you to meet' said the General as he alighted from the carriage and walked towards a small room followed by Priyu and Archika.

Inside they found the old lady who was taking care of the Prince sitting on a bench waiting for them.

Priyu and Archika immediately went to her and took her blessings. She was the oldest maid in the royal household and had raised both the Prince's from their childhood as well as their father. She was accorded the respect given to a grandmother.

'How is the Prince doing?' Archika asked her.

'It is very troubling to see my children suffer' she said 'He has started having his nightmares again and his leg is also bothering him' she paused to dab her eyes with the end of her saree. 'Why must my son suffer so?' she questioned. 'That evil witch has already taken his limb and he gave up his right to be King, what more does Almagri want from my son?' she spoke sadly her wrinkled cheeks wet and her voice weak.

Archika produced a square copper coin and placed in the hands of the old lady. 'Please keep this by the Prince's bedside or under his pillow. He will not be harmed, nor will he have nightmares' said Archika.

12. Sarpatta

12

Sarpatta

They started for the village early the next day. The ride from the capital of Oleva to the Sarpatta village would take them the entire day. As they left the once prosperous Kingdom's capital they felt that the sadness and decay of the city was also being left behind. Being in nature uplifted their mood a little and the heaviness they had felt in the city talking to the people there and the visit to the wounded man slowly drifted away. Though they felt peaceful on the solitary path their mind was occupied with the task ahead and they each contemplated the task ahead.

They decided to enter the Sarpatta village in the morning instead of the evening. They stopped at a small shrine to rest for the night and recoup their energy. The 3 of them including Doree took turns to sleep while the other kept a look out. They would reach the Sarpatta village in the morning.

Meanwhile deep in the forest the giant peered through the small window and saw the form of Kulgi sitting on the tree branch not spread out lazily like she usually was but she was perched on it. Her long tail was twitching with impatience and anticipation. Her eyes had now turned a permanent shade of green and so was the spittle that had foamed her mouth. She sat with her tongue handing out her huge canines exposed.

The giant looked down at the bowl in his hands and dreaded the task ahead. He opened the heavy door and ambled outside in his ambling gait. This time he had the bowl in one hand and the other held on to his dagger hidden in the sleeve end of his rag like robes.

Kulgi showed her displeasure at the delay made by the giant by her low growl. The giant hurried to the tree and as he bent down to place the bowl he was startled by the sudden leap of Kulgi from her perch to the ground her nose almost touching the giant's nose.

One look in the mad loathing green gaze of Kulgi and the giant backed off suddenly stumbling and spilling the bowl on the floor and with it all the contents of the magic milk that Kulgi was craving for.

The giant looked at the fallen bowl with a sudden dread and with a sinking feeling that all his nightmares of the evil Kulgi were now on the verge of actually taking place. Kulgi looked at the fallen bowl and the struggling giant just a short leap away. He saw the pupils of the beast dilated with uncontrollable anger as the green flashed in her eyes. The black and green fury leaped at the sprawled giant. Within the blink of an eye Kulgi was on the giant pinning him down to the ground her claws sinking into his shoulders. The bellow of the giant shook the leaves of the tree as he tried to shake the beast off him but the snarling Kulgi held him pinned down enjoying the misery and helplessness of the giant. The giant used all of his desperate enormous strength to bring his hands together to hold the dagger under the neck of Kulgi who was toying with the giant playing with her game before she killed it.

The sudden appearance of the dagger surprised Kulgi as the giant pushed the beast from him and in the process cut the paw of Kulgi. As Kulgi backed off and licked the blood streaming from her slashed paw the giant knew that his end was near as she circled him and charged at him with all her might. The giant was thrown to the ground with the force of the attack and he crossed his hands shielding his face from the beast in desperation who was now going for the kill.

'*Kulgi*' the command stopped the beast. The giant dared not to open his eyes, but he could feel the hot toxic breath of the beast on his face and the sharpness of the canines that had engulfed his throbbing neck which he had expected to be ripped out at any moment.

He slowly opened his eyes to see her standing at the entrance of the dwelling, one hand on her hip and the other pointed towards Kulgi. Kulgi stopped from ripping the giant's neck off but did not release the grip growling in crazed anger.

The woman took two strides towards the duo and this time her command was heard in their heads rather than been spoken out. '*Kulgi release NOW*'!

Kulgi released the giant reluctantly as the woman walked over to them and kicked the giant in the stomach 'Get up you stupid idiot' she hissed 'There is another bowl of milk, bring it before I release this beast on you'.

Kulgi cowered and backed off a little from the woman but kept snarling her blood thirsty canines at her. The giant stumbled and hurried into the dwelling to get the milk while the woman kept the snarling crazed beast at bay. The trembling giant returned back with the bowl of milk and he kept the bowl of milk carefully at the woman's feet and backed off quickly from the beast as she lapped up the milk at a feverish pace. He saw her going through her usual process of transformation as they both backed up into the dwelling and closed the door behind them on the convulsing Kulgi.

Kulgi then stood up and looked at the giant square in the eyes. The trembling giant was looking at her through the bars of the window. This time however the beast did not take off into the wild as she normally did, she crouched on the ground going round sniffing. The puzzled giant looked on as the beast sniffed around then it stopped and looked up a tree suddenly its ears twitching and it leaped into the bush climbing up the tree. The giant waited a little longer by the window puzzling over the strange behaviour of the beast when Kulgi reappeared and walked over to the window where the giant was. The giant instinctively backed up a little but he could not avert his gaze from the monster behind the bars. There was a look of arrogance and triumph on Kulgi's face as she spit out something from her mouth and shot off into the forest.

The giant peered from the window and tried to get a better look at the bloodied piece of meat on the ground but he dared not step out just yet. He looked at the thing lying on the ground and it was disturbing to the giant, he opened the door cautiously and stepped out.

A roar of anguish and despair escaped the giants lips as he saw the severed and bloodied head of his pet squirrel lying on the ground in front of the dwelling.

Toshin & Dhyum reached the outskirts of the Sarpatta village just after sunrise. Sarpatta the once prosperous agricultural belt of the Oleva Kingdom now looked deserted and desolate. More houses lay abandoned than habituated, there were no children playing on the streets, no gathering of the villagers at the village centre, no womenfolk chattering near the river bed, no sounds of worship from the once frequented temple of the forest god whom the Sarpatta villagers worshipped. An air of despair and desperation hung all around the village, even the birds seemed to have ceased their chirping here.

Toshin & Dhyum stopped at a temple at the center of the village and a few windows opened curiously to look at the new arrivals at their midst. The door of the temple which was also closed opened a little and an old man peered outside curiously. Soon a few more house doors were opened and the villagers started peering at the two men with their steads and the largest wolf they had seen walking tall and strong in the desolate village.

'Who are you sir?' the temple priest asked them from the threshold of the door. His coarse voice was tired and weak.

'We want to talk to the village head' Toshin announced.

He now opened the temple door fully and a thin frail man walked out to the courtyard gingerly.

'What is about?' he asked hesitantly studying the fine armory and the men closely.

A few of the men had ventured to take a closer look at the new arrivals, their women stayed near the door holding their curious children back.

'We will bring him here' the priest said before they could answer as he sent his young son to the Village head's house. The young boy ran to a house nearby followed by a couple of kids his size.

By now a few more old men from the village and a few curious women had joined him. They closed in cautiously on the two fine young warriors in their midst. They watched in awe at the armaments they wore and the confidence and poise in which they carried themselves.

All of a sudden there was a flurry of activity in the village as a few charpai's (a traditionally woven bed) were placed in the temples yard, more men, women and children filled in the temple courtyard. It looked as though the entire village or what was left of the village had filled into that yard.

They looked at the new arrivals expectantly and asked them to sit on the furniture placed. Someone gave them water to drink as the rest of the villagers gathered around the hunters and squatted in the front yard looking at them attentively. The young ones and the elders alike were transfixed by the strange armory of the two men and stared to admire and wonder about them.

Soon another village elder walked into the courtyard tying his turban as he hurriedly joined the priest and they sat on the charpai facing Toshin & Dhyum.

'Welcome to Sarpatta, how can we help you?' The Village elder spoke. The old man's turban suggested a high stature in the village but his lined troubled face spoke defeat and gloominess

'We have heard that you are being troubled by a beast and that you are giving a reward for killing it' spoke out Toshin addressing the assembled villagers. 'We are hunters from the Ajoori clan of mount Bindu and we will kill the beast and claim our reward.'

There was a murmur within the assembled villagers

'I have heard of the Ajoori's' he said. 'The Ajoori's are known for being great hunters but alas I do not think even you can help us son.' He spoke sadly.

'Why do you say that?' asked Toshin as Dhyum looked on.

'Because what is troubling us is not a beast of flesh and blood but it is the devil itself' he said to the murmured approval of the gathered villagers.

'We have come across many devils in our hunts' spoke Dhyum 'and we have yet to come across a devil that did not bleed.'

'So we will destroy it and collect our reward?' said Toshin.

'Look around you son' he said 'what you see is a bunch of people who are cursed to die here. Those who could leave Sarpatta have already left leaving behind only us the sick, the old and the hopeless. Even the King and our gods have forsaken us. Why else has our protector 'Mitrumai' unleased this beast on us?' He was referring to their deity 'Mitru' the forest goddess. 'We pray for your success and if you both succeed then all that we have is yours' he said.

Toshin & Dhyum looked at the deity of the goddess in the temple and saluted the deity before continuing 'Why have you not been able to kill the beast?' asked Toshin.

'Because the beast belongs to the evil Rohini sorceress' a young boy spoke up and he was immediately shushed by the villagers. 'Do not say her name' he was scolded by the terrified villagers.

'why not? It is true' he protested 'I have seen her…the witch' he spoke with eagerness before being silenced by his mother again.

'And what did you see?' Dhyum encouraged the boy to speak.

The boy looked towards his mother and the village elder who nodded his approval to speak.

'I was grazing our goats' he started 'I only grace on this side of the mountain but our usual gracing land was dry because Dhurru graces his cattle there continuously without a break' he pointed accusingly at Dhurru another boy of his age who was sitting with his father. 'That is not correct' cried Dhurru's father angrily standing up 'That land has always been for cattle, my father did it and before that my grandfather and many generations before that'.

This got in an angry response from the boy's mother 'But you have always washed your cattle upriver, where we wash our clothes' she scolded him angrily.

This provoked Dhurru's mother in joining in the fray and in no time half of the gathered villagers were squabbling over old disputes.

'Quiet everyone…quiet' the Village elder spoke up, standing and silencing the villagers.

'What is the matter with you people?' he scolded them 'The first time we get an opportunity to gather like this in such a long time and you fight among each other like in a time like this?' he spoke to the now silent villagers.

He looked at the drawn tired faces of the gathered and remarked 'Actually we have not had a good argument in a long time too' he laughed out aloud with the villagers joining in the laughter. 'and we have not had a good laugh too' he said in a bitter sweet smile.

'I don't know who you are and how you came to know of our plight and honestly we do not want to see fine men like you risking your lives for us but we do not have a choice here' he said apologetically to them.

'You were telling us about the sorceress?' said Dhyum waving away the concerns of the old man and bringing the topic back to the sorceress.

'There are some plantain trees which my goats like, so I had taken them to eat plantains when I heard a strange cry so I went to see what it was. I went quietly because I was scared' the boy recounted 'I crept to the edge of the plantain groove and peeked down into the witch's house.'

This earned him a whack on his head from his mother 'I told you a hundred times not to go there.'

'But you have already beaten me for this' the boy complained to his mother rubbing his head.

'So what did you see there?' Dhyum encouraged the boy to continue with his story.

'Go on, continue your story…' his mother swiped at him again but this time the boy was prepared and ducked the blow to the annoyance of his mother. He got up and moved closer to the front away from the trigger happy hands of his mother who instead whacked his younger brother when he laughed at the missed swipe by his mother.

The boy now turned to the engrossed villagers listening to his tale 'So I crept to the edge of the plantation and I peeped down at the witches layer' he said turning to the little kids with widened eyes as they cowered in their mother's lap.

'And I saw the most terrifying man ever. He was as tall as a mountain and just as wide' he paused for dramatic effect.

'But last time you had said he was as tall as a banyan tree' a little boy corrected him.

'Quiet' the young story teller quietened the young boy and continued with his story 'This giant had a pet in a cage' he said turning to Toshin & Dhyum.

'What sort of pet?' Toshin asked.

'It was a black spotted tiger, as dark and as black as the night' the boy uttered to the hush of the gathered villagers. 'That's the demon' the villagers chorused.

'So it is definitely a black leopard, not a stripped tiger' Dhyum conferred with Toshin.

'What was the giant doing with the black beast?' he asked the boy.

'The giant was feeding it' the boy said 'At first it gave it a fowl which the beast gobbled up and then the giant gave it some milk to drink and when it didn't drink, he started laughing and pocking the black tiger with a stick' the boy paused here, visibly scared.

'And…' Toshin urged the boy to continue.

'That is when I saw her…when the black tiger was not drinking the milk the evil witch came out of the house and the tiger started drinking the milk immediately'

'What did she do for the beast to drink the milk? Did she beat it or do something else?' asked Dhyum all attention.

'No she whispered in the beast's ear to start drinking or else she will eat its cubs.'

'You say she whispered in the beasts ears and still you could hear it?' asked Dhyum

'Yes, I could hear it clearly even from far, it was like she was talking inside my head'

Dhyum and Toshin exchanged glances.

'What happened next?' Toshin asked.

'The black tiger drank the milk and I thought that it was going to die the way it was struggling on the floor of the cage, while the giant laughed at it, poking it with the stick. I got scared and I ran away from there taking my goats with me.' he said.

'What did she look like?' asked Dhyum

The boy gave them a blank look 'I don't remember' he said.

Toshin & Dhyum exchanged glances again, finally they asked the villagers 'Where do you think we can find this beast?'

The village elder spoke 'Once you are in the jungle the beast will find you.'

13. Battle Ready

13

Battle Ready

Toshin & Dhyum had discussed in length what they had just heard from the villagers and they had understood a few things. Firstly, they were hunting a large black leopard and not a tiger as everyone claimed. This made their task even more difficult as the black leopard is one of the most elusive creatures of the wild and sighting it at night would be a challenge. From the description and stories heard about it, this beast was far more dangerous than the normal leopard, so they will have to be on their guard at all times.

They had also gathered that this beast had made its kill only at night, so it must be resting somewhere during the day. The intriguing part was that this leopard was not behaving like leopards do. It was killing at random and even when it was not hungry, which was rare for a wild beast to put itself in danger by hunting when it was not hungry. That left them wondering what was done to it by the sorceress and the giant that had turned this beast into an unpredictable man-eater. The part of the leopard being a man-eater disturbed them the most as they it may very well turn out that they are the ones who are hunted.

It was high noon when they made a quick reconnaissance of the forest on the outskirts of the village. It was a thick rainforest with a lush green canopy of rosewood and teak. Clumps of bamboo were found near the stream and it was blessed with rains almost the entire year. The density of the forest gave both the hunted and the hunter ample camouflage.

They quickly found the trees that the leopard frequented. They studied the pug marks and the scratches marks confirmed what they had earlier suspected, that the leopard was a female and much heavier than a normal leopard.

'Do you see something strange in these marks here?' asked Dhyum pointing to the scratch marks on the tree to Toshin.

'You see these marks are fresh down here but the scratches on top are old ones.' he remarked.

'Why do you think, she is not climbing the tree anymore?' asked Toshin

'Could it be that she is getting heavier to climb trees? Let us find out a few more trees that the beast frequents' said Dhyum and they found a few more trees found the same pattern of the marks. The leopard was not climbing trees now as all the climb marks were old and no fresh marks above a certain height was found. They also found a pattern to the frequency of kills from some of the carcasses found in the forest.

The evening was approaching now as the sun began its descent. They had moved deeper into the forest studying the lay of the land planning their hunt. The villagers had come only to the outskirts of the jungle and had allowed them to cross the small stream and head on their own with Doree for company.

Dhyum & Toshin had kept their ears open to listen to the call of birds and the monkeys who often sent alarm calls to warn of the presence of beast. He sensed that Doree had picked up some movement and was alert 'What is it?' he asked Doree.

Doree kept looking at the woods ahead not moving 'Do you see something Doree?' asked Dhyum as both of them readied their weapons.

Doree gave a low growl as they saw movement in the bushes ahead of them Dhyum had his bow ready and Toshin had his spear as they both braced themselves.

Doree gave a woof as a big black boar shot out from the bush rushing towards them. Dhyum let go of two quick arrows at the oncoming boar as the boar skidded to a stop near them motionless, his arrows buried deep in the boar's neck. Toshin quickly moved to the dying beast and put it out of its misery.

'We got bait' said Toshin. They carried half of their kill to the village to spend the night and prepare for the hunt the next day.

That night there was a renewed energy in the village as they jostled to host the warriors who had come into the village like a ray of hope. Though Toshin and Dhyum had made no promises it did not bother the villagers as the hope starved villagers were looking to snatch any small piece of optimism that presented itself and celebrate that moment. After a very long time they had all gathered in the village chieftain's courtyard at night to dine with the guests. Each of the women had cooked their best meal and they wore their finest cloth and jewelry and the men wore their finest turbans and came out with oiled mustaches. Together they would defy the sorceress and the beast tonight. They would celebrate the night with music, food and laughter for now.

The next morning they gathered a few of the remaining men and returned to set some traps near the trees they found the most pug marks. They worked quickly keeping in mind the light as the nervous villagers wanted to return back well before sunset.

The villagers had worked through the night in the village preparing a strong bamboo wall for Toshin and Dhyum to stay behind. They had chosen a spot facing a huge rock. It gave them some measure of protection if they had their back against the rock, at least the beast could not attack them from behind.

They erected the canopy made of sturdy bamboo which they had fastened with a tightly woven twine. They camouflaged it with leaves and fixed it against the rock. Now the hunters had a small degree of protection against the might of the beast. It was nearing evening and the forest became alive with the sunset call of the birds as they made their way back to their perch.

The villagers stopped and listened to the forest. It was time for them to return to safety. They quickly collected their tools and went over to the two warriors. They hugged them full of hope and trepidation and headed back to their village.

It was a full moon night and that gave them enough light without having to resort to their torches.

The bait of the boar meat was placed on the trees they had seen the leopard markings. They had selected a spot for the wait depending on which direction the wind was blowing. When the villagers had left Toshin and Dhyum quickly checked the traps again and crawled behind the small defensive partition wall the villagers had made for them. Though not fully safe it gave the hunters some protection between the hunter and the hunted and they could shoot their arrows through the gaps.

14. The Hunter and the Hunted

14

The Hunter and the Hunted

The two hunters and Doree began the wait behind the concealed hideout for the arrival of the beast. They wore full light weight armour along with neck braces, even Doree had a neck brace with spikes on it to thwart off attack on the neck. The villagers had spread dried grass around the area so that they could be alerted of any movement in the area.

Dhyum uncorked a small vail and took a deep sniff from it and passed it to Toshin who did likewise. They closed their eyes and waited for the potion to take effect, they could now feel the potion work its magic as one by one their senses were on high alert and their mind clear.

Kulgi got up from her sleep and yawned. She was not sleeping well these days. Ever since she had got accustomed to the magic milk her sleep has been disturbed and often woke up with a splitting headache and sometimes she had no memory of what had happened the previous night.

Today was such a day, she woke up with a sore throbbing head and she moved her head very slowly to avoid quick movements which would make the pain acute. She had even stopped climbing trees because of the heavy head and that made her lose her balance.

She licked at her blood stained paw and remembered the giant slashing at her paw with his dagger. She placed her paw gingerly on the floor and a pain shot up through her front paw and she raged in pain. The giant's days are numbered she promised herself.

The giant sat at his favourite spot near the barn with a handful of sunflower seeds in his big palm. His tears fell on the seeds making his palms wet. He dropped the seeds with a sigh and stood up with difficulty.

'Oleg' she heard him call, 'Come here darling' she said sweetly, but there was no warmth in her tone.

He ambled slowly to the dwelling, his wounds inflicted by Kulgi was still raw and the gash in his shoulder had started festering. He entered the chamber with the tub and found that the tub was full with a white concoction similar to the milk they used to feed Kulgi, the woman was busy stirring it.

'Maybe you could move just a little bit slower' she added sarcastically with the same tone at him 'Bring me water in this' she pointed at a large cauldron 'and go to the yard and bring all the fowls that are there.'

The giant stood there uncertain 'Kulgi...' he mumbled.

'What?' she asked busy with stirring her pot and adding some potion and powder to it.

'Kulgi...kill my pet...' he mumbled with difficulty

'Get started now' she said slowly, it was more like a snarl and he knew better than to face the consequences of disobeying her orders.

As he turned to go out he saw the monitor lizard appear at the window and slide in towards her. She stopped and waited patiently for the giant to make his way out of the room. As he closed the door he thought he heard whispers.

He walked slowly to the back yard to collect the fowls when he heard his name again, he turned back and saw the woman standing in the back yard 'Bring me the Raven NOW' she screamed.

King Oleva stood on his balcony and looked out at the city in front of him. The evening sun was just setting and the orange red glow cast a gloomy mood on the city. He looked at the monuments erected in the Town square which were once proud reminders of their many conquests and victories now they were a grave reminder of the hard times they were facing.

The town streets, monuments and temples were badly in need of rebuilding and maintenance. The streets were hardly cleaned and the cobble stones were not re-laid, the garbage and refuse were not collected regularly and moss and decay was growing in every corner of the city.

We will be a proud nation again he promised himself. We will have chariot races and festivals again. We will have traders coming back and neighbouring Kingdoms respecting us again. You ignore us now, but for how long? I will make you pay for their insults, starting with you Smikruta and you Brihu imbecile of Almagri he thought, clenching his fist. The patch on his face started burning when he thought of the prince Brihu of Almagri and of the day when he had received this mark on his face as a reminder of his failure 'You will Pay' he vowed himself.

The King was lost in his thoughts when the cawing of a raven caught his ears and he turned to look at a raven that had landed on his balcony and tied to its feet was a rolled up piece of cloth.

He unrolled the piece of parchment and read the message 'Guard, bring me the Commander of the Kings Guards' he thundered.

Kulgi walked through the jungle, she was hungry, she was hurt and she was angry. She was in no mood or state to hunt game today. With this headache and torn paw they would easily outrun her. No, she decided it's time to pay that village another visit. They still had some cattle she thought to herself. If not cattle I might just have to do with human flesh till I feel better she consoled herself.

She made her way painfully towards the stream which she would have to cross to get to the village. She heard the call of the langur above her. Damn that monkey she cursed it, the only reason that monkey is chirping is because it knows I am not climbing trees anymore.

She sniffed in the air and caught a faint smell of boar meat. She followed the smell, the alarm call of a few more langur monkey's startled the birds as they echoed their own calls of alarm.

'Listen' Toshin nudged a meditating Dhyum as they heard the alarm calls of the jungle. Doree perked up and sat straight looking intently towards the forest from their cover.

Dhyum picked up his bow and arrow slowly without making a sound and Toshin tightened his grip on his spear in his right hand his dagger in his left.

Kulgi followed the scent and quickly deduced that it was indeed boar. Its hunger drove it to the spot. She stopped and sniffed in the night air, there was another scent in the air. It intrigued her, there was a strange beast she was not familiar with and its scent was mixed with the scent of the dead boar.

The Kulgi of the past would have been cautious and investigated the area further. It would have climbed a high branch and taken a good aerial view of the place and it would have waited patiently for the prey to make a false move and then it would weigh the options to eighter pounce or give up the hunt but this was not the old Kulgi, now she was the queen of the jungle. No one could dare stand against her and if they were foolish enough to try and face her, it would be to their peril.

She reached the clearing near the stream and she could see the meat hanging on the tree branch and this irritated her further. Her paw was paining, and she had not climbed for quite some time now. She looked at the bait closely and tried to sniff again at the strange scent that was coming to her and then she heard it, the slight rustling sound of movement. She turned her attention from the meat hanging above to a spot near the large rock.

She froze still all her senses were on high alert as she saw carefully at every tree, bush and rock through her highly developed night time vision. And then there it was again a whisper, a gasping of breath and she saw the dull glow of an object as the arrow from Dhyum's bow screamed towards her. She was able to leap just in time as the arrow missed her neck and instead glanced through her shoulder cutting it.

Two more arrows flew out of the bow in quick succession as she successfully avoided it rushing to the spot where the arrows came from. She pounded on the bamboo partition with all her might, the bamboo partition was no match for the powerful jaws and neck muscles of the cat as it grabbed the bamboo cover and shook it apart with anger.

Dhyum and Toshin thrust their sword and spear at the enraged cat as it tried to tear apart the bamboo cover. Their spear and sword thrust only made some minor cuts and it would only be a matter time before there would be no defence between them.

Part of the partition had already crumbled and it was enough gap for Doree to climb through and attack the rampaging Kulgee. Doree attacked the cat from behind and tried to get a grip of its hind legs. Kulgi was surprised at the sudden appearance of the wolf. She had never seen a wolf before and had never encountered any animal ready to take on Kulgi apart from the silly humans who had learnt their lesson.

She let go of the bamboo partition and looked at the strange dog holding on to his hind leg. He shook her off easily as she sprung up and landed softly. She took a good look at

Doree as she crouched snarling at this big dog stupid enough to face the might of Kulgi, the queen of the jungle.

Her green eyes flared in anger as she pounced on Doree going for the neck. Dhyum and Toshin were out of their cover and they rushed towards the struggling duo as they rolled on the floor slashing and swiping at each other snarling and ripping at each other's throat.

Doree was saved for the fact that she had her neck brace to protect her for the moment but the wild cat's powerful bite was threatening to cut through the brace at any moment now as it caught Doree in its wise like grip and shook it like a puppy.

Seeing Doree in trouble Dhyum leaped at the cat with a war cry and landed on its back with his dagger out and tried to sink his dagger into its belly, he was shocked by the strength of the cat as it swatted away Doree like an irritating fly and faced Dhyum with its evil eyes. He was momentarily transfixed by the green ferociousness of the beast as it locked eyes with him. Dhyum realized that he had lost his dagger in the scuffle with the beast and faced the beast with his bare hands as it leaped at him and they both rolled to the ground, Dhyum trying to protect his face and neck and Kulgi slashing at him wildly.

Toshin lunged at the beast with his spear as it sat upon Dhyum. Dhyum was struggling to keep the jaws of death away from him when Toshin struck at its belly with his spear with all his might.

The beast gave a shriek of pain as the spear pierced its skin. Toshin drew back his spear and preparing for the next blow when Kulgi lunged at his spear hand. Doree was up and attacked the big cat from behind. Kulgi was now bleeding profusely from the cut in her belly and shoulder. It swiped at Toshin and Doree snarling at them and they were tiring fast. Doree had a limp on its front paw and Toshin was cut badly on his legs and arms from the fangs and claws of Kulgi. And Kulgi though cut was fighting to the finish with a mad intensity.

Toshin took a quick glance at the motionless figure of Dhyum and that is when Kulgi also caught his eyes and turned towards the prone figure of Dhyum and turned towards him. A chill went through Toshin when he realised the intent in Kulgi was to attack the unconscious Dhyum and jumped her with his dagger drawn and attacked her belly the same area repeatedly stabbing where his spear had wounded her. Kulgi leaped high in the air escaping Toshin's dagger and Toshin was also thrown to the ground.

A gasping Kulgi turned towards Toshin who was now covering his prone friend and put himself between Dhyum and the beast clutching his dagger in his left hand, his right hand was severely cut and bruised. Doree also limped towards her master and stood next to Toshin, ready to protect her fallen master with her life.

Kulgi tried to stand up straight on all four but winced in the effort, its paw was badly cut and she could not place it on the ground without a jolt of pain shooting up her limbs. She tried to hobble towards Toshin and Doree when something stopped her in her tracks. It was the unmistaken aroma of the one thing that Kulgi craved.

Kulgi looked around wildly around and then she saw the thick foliage part and the huge silhouette of the giant came into view. The giant stood there and took in the whole scene. He looked at the prone form of Dhyum, the mountain wolf standing guard over the prone hunter and an equally bruised and bloodied hunter protecting them. He saw the splatter of blood and tuffs of skin and hair around him and then his eyes slowly fell on Kulgi and his face hardened.

He slowly and dramatically raised his right hand for Kulgi to see. He held a bowl in his extended raised hand. He took a step from the foliage towards them and stepped into the clearing facing them.

The giant stood there with the bowl of the magic milk in his hands. Kulgi turned away from Toshin and hobbled slowly towards the magic milk. It was a now a broken and damaged Kulgi that walked towards the giant, pleading and desperation in her eyes. She was no longer the queen demanding her right, she was a broken addict begging for her salvation. The giant savored his moment of triumph as for once the scales had turned in his favour and it was the beast Kulgi who was at his mercy. He put his head back and roared in laughter and satisfaction.

With an effort Kulgi had managed to hobble and drag her way to the giant when to the amazement of Toshin the giant waved the bowl of milk mockingly at Kulgi and as she was within sniffing distance to them the giant tilted the bowl and poured all the liquid on the ground to the growing anguish of Kulgi. She leapt to the spot ignoring her pain and tried to lick the spilled milk when the giant roared in laughter at the misery of Kulgi.

As the giant roared in celebration beating his chest there was a slow change in Kulgi as she became very still and quiet. Toshin instinctively picked up his spear and steadied himself. Kulgi looked at the giant and now the giant too was also deadly silent as they both looked at each other. The giant had his dagger in his hands as they lunged at each other with such a mighty roar that the leaves in the forest shook for miles.

Kulgi straight away went for the jugular as the giant caught the leaping leopard in his enormous grip. They both hit the ground hard and there was a brief struggle. Toshin watched them as Kulgi fell on top of the giant her canines sunk deep into his throat and the giants dagger buried deep into her heart.

All of the sudden it was all over. The frantic pace of the battle right from the appearance of Kulgi to struggle with the giant must have lasted all of 10 minutes, but it looked like an eternity as the two fallen giants lay upon each other motionless and silent in an eternal embrace of death.

15. The Last Stand

15

The Last Stand

The chief of the King's Guards appeared before King Oleva at his reception room. He bowed and waited for the King to address him. The King looked at him steadfast smoking his shisha (tobacco water pipe also known as the Hookah) as the Chief waited patiently not making a move.

'You' he said pointing his finger at the Kings guard 'I believe, *You* are in charge of the security of the Kingdom?' he said at last behind a cloud of vapour that escaped his lips. His voice was level and calm but there was no denying the suppressed rage.

Though it was framed as a question, the guard was silent. He stood there, head bowed.

'Answer me' the King said slowly.

'Yes, your Majesty' the Chief answered anxious to know where this was leading.

'I presume you would know any breach that happens in the Kingdom?'

'Yes your Majesty, we are on high alert. All the borders have been secured'

'So I ask you, then what must I do with you if you fail your job?' he asked steadily and evenly enjoying the discomfort of the chief.

'I apologise your Majesty, I do not know what you are referring to' he stuttered.

'What do you know then?' he looked around at the room. There were a few of his ministers, his chief of staff, his personal guards, his defense minister and a few others present.

'I am surrounded by fools' he spat out to the nervous bunch, some of them shifted in their chairs uncomfortably. 'Your right hand doesn't know, what your left is doing' he bellowed out to the silent audience, his voice raising with each syllable.

His rough purple patch of skin began itching violently as he called for his assistant irritably. She quickly walked up to him with a bowl in a tray and applied a white cream on the wound cooling it.

'Enough' he screamed pushing her aside roughly scattering the bowl with its contents on the floor.

'Enough of your incompetence' he screamed at no one and at everyone in the room.

'There is a war looming on us, I hope you are aware of that' he spoke pointedly to his Chief.

The maid hurriedly picked up the fallen bowl and scampered out of the room while the others maintained silence.

He looked at his chief of staff for a while 'hmm, what will I do with you?' he mused wearily.

The chief stole a quick glance at the King. The King had a smirk on his face which was not good for me, the chief thought but at the same time the King also looked tired, which could be in my favour the chief prayed fervently.

The King was known to chop off heads for much lesser offences that one of national security. He had to muster all of his courage and all of his will power not to tremble in front of the audience.

The King sighed and spoke at length 'Dismiss the fool from duty, he will be a foot soldier from today' he declared waving him away. In normal times I would surely have had this fools head the King thought to himself, but with the war preparations I would need every hand. Also having the Chief executed or imprisoned would probably affect the morale of the army and no I don't want another headache at the moment.

The chief of guards was very relieved to be led out of the room, his head intact.

The King turned to his court advisor, a wily old veteran and spoke to him 'Your nephew, what's his name?'

'Morin, your Majesty' he answered hurriedly. Standing up as straight as his bent back could.

'"Morin your Majesty" what sort of stupid name is that?' the King looked at him.

'It is just "Morin"…umm your Majesty'

The King looked at him in distaste for a while smoking his shisha. He blew a ring and said 'Old man, you always wanted your nephew in that position, appoint this 'Moron' as the new Chief of the King's Guard' he commanded.

'Your Majesty…um…its not…'

'Yes?' the King asked him irritation mounting.

'Nothing important your Majesty, would you like to meet 'Moron'…I mean Morin?'

'Yes' the King sighed bored with the conversation 'Bring him to me now'.

Morin the new Chief of the Kings Guards stood in front of the King, straight backed and eager to please the King.

'It is an honour, your Majesty, a great privilege…'

'Listen here carefully' the King interrupted him, 'Your uncle here' he looked towards the smiling hook nosed uncle and looked away quickly towards the beaming hook nosed nephew 'your uncle has been pushing your name for this position for a while now' he paused to take a deep breath of his shisha and continued 'Now is your chance to show how much of what your uncle said is true.'

'Yes your Majesty, I will endeavour to…'

'Shhh' the King shushed him

'You people' he looked from Uncle to nephew 'Is this a family trait? Of talking nonstop?'

'No…ofcourse not your Majesty' the uncle jumped in 'He will *Listen* and do your bidding, your Majesty' he emphasized the word 'Listen' as he spoke to the King but looking at his nephew.

'Now look here' the King addressed the new Chief 'You know where the Sarpatta forest is?' he asked him.

'Very well your Majesty, I have been there many times. Twice with you to…' he stopped adding anything further.

'Good' the King said 'I hear of some disturbance there. Some hunters have entered the jungle there and have been hunting and creating a disturbance there. Go there and find out who these hunters are, how and when did they come into our Kingdom without our knowledge' he said angrily before adding 'Find them and bring them to me' he said.

'Very well your Majesty, your command will….'

The King left his seat before he could finish his sentence.

Priyu walked quickly towards the Kings private meeting chambers. He reached the door and stopped to catch his breath when the guard announced him in and admitted him to the King's chambers. He was relieved to see Fauja already present there.

They exchanged greetings even though they had spent the better half of the day together. Customs and tradition was important to Priyu in a formal meeting and even the King made a point to observe these in the presence of his Chief Minister.

Once the formalities were over, he waited for the King to address him.

'Tell us dear Priyu, good tidings I pray?' the King enquired.

'Glory to the Sun god and Glory to Almagri, I do have some good news and some not so good news' Priyu said.

'Go on' the King pressed him.

'The good news is, my men have cleared the first hurdle. They have been successful in eliminating a beast and a giant that were guarding the sorceress. It was believed that the beast a black leopard was possessed by an evil spirit and had turned into such a menace that no one even dared to enter the forest, but my brave men have not only eliminated the beast but also a personal bodyguard of the sorceress a human giant' said Priyu proudly.

'Well done' the King and the General offered their congratulations.

'Your men are okay? They are not hurt I hope' the King offered.

'Not grievously your Majesty, but yes one of them is unwell and needs attention' Priyu added.

'And the beasts that carried them?' the King asked referring to their horses.

'They are fine, your Majesty' Priyu answered straight faced.

'Glory be to Almagri' the King applauded 'Now tell us the bad news'.

'The Rohini is vulnerable now as her protectors have gone but King Oleva has sent in a company of soldiers to protect her and they have started looking for our men.'

'And your men are…' the General asked.

'…are safe for now' Priyu said 'I have moved them to a safe place for the injured to rest and recuperate before we plan our next move'.

'How much time do we have?' the General asked.

'Not much time I am afraid' said Priyu 'King Oleva has organized an 'Austro' and you know when an Austro is performed they must start before the flame from the Austro pyre dies'.

'Can we somehow postpone the Austro?' asked the King.

'I am working on it' said Priyu.

'There is another thing that has been bothering me' said the King 'There is someone who is supporting Oleva from outside, where else does he get the money for the war?'

'I have been looking in it and we will get an idea soon' said the minister 'But for the moment I need my men safe and I need them to complete the task at hand'.

'Let us pray for their success' said the King gravely.

It was now the second day after the slaying of the beast. Toshin had managed to somehow half carry and half drag the gravely wounded Dhyum back to the village.

The villagers had rushed to help the wounded warriors and received them back in the village as heroes and had showered them with gratitude and affection. They tried to make them as comfortable as they could and village astrologer who double as the medic had dressed up their wounds to the best of his knowledge. Even Doree was treated for her wounds and her broken paw.

The next morning a group of the King's guards had marched into the village looking for the hunters. The villagers and the King's guards had no love lost between them especially since the King had ignored their plight and had instead hid the two warriors and had feigned ignorance about the whereabouts of the hunters. The depleted village had decided to protect their saviors at all cost. The beast and the Kings sorceress had cost them enough young men, life stock and loss of livelihood and now the King wanted to punish the very men who had saved them from an agonizing slow death and they decided to pit their loyalty with the young hunters. The soldiers had searched all the houses of the village and had come out empty handed.

The artifacts merchant had come to the village and had made arrangements along with the help of the villagers to hide the two hunters in an old shrine that was abandoned and lay crumbling.

Toshin looked at the unwell face of Dhyum, his fever had not come down for the last two days and the wounds on his shoulder and abdomen seemed festering and growing worse. He was in and out of consciousness and seemed to mumble incoherently.

'He needs help' a troubled Toshin implored the artifacts merchant. 'He is not going to last long if nothing is done'.

'How can we take him to the city?' the merchant pondered. 'The roads are watched and he is too sick to be moved, the journey itself would kill him'

'Why didn't she come?' shouted an angry Toshin 'You should have forced her to come here'.

Toshin was referring to the monk of the Austrom, he had sent for her through the merchant.

'Toshin, I understand your pain son' the merchant tried to pacify Toshin 'What she did was for the best, trust me. The roads are watched so closely that I could barely get through. The King had come to know that you had travelled with the monks, they are also under very close watch. This King is crazy as well as paranoid. We decided that we will certainly give your location away if she comes here. That's why she had sent the medications instead of coming herself or sending someone.'

'But her medicines are not working' cried Toshin

'I know son' the merchant thought to himself, maybe that is why the monk decided not to come, she has no cure for such deadly poison.

'She has told you to look out for foaming in the mouth and erratic behavior if and when he wakes up…it's a bad sign' he could not say that it meant the end is near.

'There is one thing she told me to tell you as a last resort', the merchant ventured hesitantly.

'Tell me' cried Toshin.

'Now, you think this as a crazy idea, but believe me even I felt the same when she told me this.'

'For gods sake, just tell me' Toshin implored.

'She suggested that you ask the sorceress for help' he blurted out.

Toshin stared stunned at the merchant, not believing what he had just heard.

'What??' he screamed incredulously, 'Are you out of your mind, old man?'

The merchant held out both his hands 'This is HER suggestion, not mine'

'This is beyond stupid, why will she help us?....why will the sorceress cure Dhyum?' he cried, his voice getting higher.

'That sorceress is the reason why he is like that? Look at him? This is not a normal bite. That infection is not curable, this is a poisoned animal bite, why will she agree to cure him?'

They sat in silence, each brooding over the topic. Toshin looked at the motionless Dhyum who was breathing heavily. His breaths came out in gasps. The wounded and troubled wolf looked sadly at her master, staying close to him.

The merchant stood up wearily 'I have to go now, Toshin' he said softly.

'I will be back with more medicines and food as soon as I can. You should get some rest too, you have not slept a wink the last 2 days. Your wounds need healing too' he told a dejected Toshin.

The merchant stopped at the door and looked back 'Toshin' he called him 'Don't lose hope son, there is always hope'.

When Toshin did not respond he continued 'If not willingly she might help unwillingly' he said as he departed.

Toshin took a deep breath and tried to calm himself down. He set his mind on attending to Dhyum. He remembered the instructions she had relayed through the merchant.

He first checked for improvements in the skin colour of Dhyum which was still a dull grey, his temperature was still high and his eyes had started collecting gunk. He picked the bottle of leaches she had sent and carefully pulled out some worms with a stick and placed them on the many wounds of Dhyum.

He watched as the Leaches bloated sucking up the blood from the wounds of Dhyum, they turned blue and dropped off.

He kept changing the cool wet cloth he had covered his chest and head with and kept cleaning him with the wet cloth. He then cleaned the wounds by removing the puss that had formed and applying the ointment that the woman monk had sent.

All this while Dhyum hardly made any movements. He fed a broth which he promptly vomited out. Toshin was running out of options, tired he sat down next to Dhyum thinking of what the merchant had told him.

He thought of the faceless sorceress. How would she be? How did she talk, walk? Did she sleep? What was the food she ate? What motivates her? What scares her?

A face came to his mind, it was a woman who stood in the distance and he was drifting towards her. He was drifting in waves, up and down. In the distance he saw a warrior on a horse. The warrior had a wolf with him. The warrior was young, strong and handsome. They both were riding towards the woman who was floating on a cloud of mist. Her feet was not visible. As the warrior and the wolf reached the woman, she turned to Toshin and he saw her face change. Her eyes were growing apart and they were turning smaller, her nose, ears and hair disappeared and her mouth was stretching into a wide slit. She was shrinking and her skin was growing scales. As the warrior approached her she transformed into a large reptile and escaped in the cloud mist.

As Toshin looked on the warrior reached him, he was no longer a young man but a young boy and there was something very familiar about him and he was saying something to Toshin.

Toshin tried to make sense of what he was saying, it was a faint echo 'Follow the lizard….follow the lizard…'

Toshin woke up with a start and looked at the sleeping Dhyum next to him. His hands were gripping Toshin hard and his mouth was foaming.

Early morning the next day, Toshin found the boy who had seen the sorceress's dwelling in the jungle. The boy led him to the banana plantation that was above the dwelling and from here they could get an uninterrupted view of the full place. They moved to the edge and Toshin peeped down and he saw the backyard of the foreboding looking house. It was a desolate place with pieces of junk strewn all over the place. There was a pit which looked like it was brimming with a green coloured molten liquid, animal skins and bones were strewn all around and there was a pile of what looked like animal innards in another corner. When the breeze blew he smelt decay and death from the gloomy dwelling below.

He sent the boy back and kept his watch patiently. In regular intervals he saw a two man patrol circling the yard. He counted a total of eight soldiers. There was a barn a little ahead and he guessed the other two soldiers resting there when the two on duty kept guard.

He continued is watch waiting to get a glimpse of the sorceress when something caught his eye on one of the windows. A head of a monitor lizard appeared and it quietly slid out of the window. It was a strange large reptile and he had never come across such a reptile before, but there was something very familiar about it. He took a deep intake of breath when he realized it was the same reptile he had seen in his dream. The words 'Follow the lizard' came to his mind as he quietly made his way down and hid himself waiting for the reptile to cross him.

Soon the reptile ambled across him unaware of Toshin's presence. Toshin kept a safe distance and followed the reptile. The reptile made its way deeper in the forest. At regular intervals it would stop and looked around as if to make sure that there was no one around, but Toshin quietly kept track of the reptile as he saw it approach a huge termite mound. It was a huge termite mound and it towered over him like a tree. He saw the reptile go behind the mound.

Toshin stayed in hidding for a while and when the reptile did not reappear he carefully rounded the mound looking for the reptile, but there was no sign of the reptile anywhere. It had just disappeard behind the mound.

It was getting dark and Toshin lit his torch fire and magnified the light using his reflective stone. He placed the torch on a rock and got down close to the ground to inspecting the marks of the reptile and realized that it had entered the termite mound.

Instinct told Toshin to look behind him immediately and he was just in time to see the reptile sneak up on him from behind.

Toshin was ready as he quickly rolled out of the way and stood up facing the hissing reptile as it waited to strike at him. Toshin looked warily at the thick saliva formed at the mouth of the large reptile, he had learnt that the poisonous saliva of the monitor lizard was potent enough to kill huge buffaloes and though big in size the reptile was quick and venomous. He pointed his spear at it to keep it at bay.

The reptile did not move from the mound and a sudden thought went into Toshin's mind, he realized that the reptile was guarding the mound. There has to be something precious in the mound to the reptile for it guard it and that could be only thing though Toshin.

He hastily gathered some dry leaves around the mound and lit it on fire. The angry reptile hissed as the fire slowly spread near the mound and it sprang inside the termite mound. Toshin waited outside the mound as it reappeared carrying two eggs in its mouth. It placed the eggs a little away from the mound and jumped back into the mound again.

The lizard piled a total of 6 eggs from the mound and lay down in exhaustion from inhaling the fumes. Toshin was waiting for this opportunity as he quickly put a noose around the lizards head and secured the other end to a tree. He pulled the leash tighter as the struggling reptile was pulled closer to the tree and away from the eggs it was protecting.

'Got you' said an exhausted Toshin as scooped up the eggs carefully in his arms. The angry reptile was now struggling with all its might to free itself and the trashing of its powerful neck was shaking the very tree.

Toshin knew he had very less time as the powerful jaws of the reptile would cut through the rope any moment now. He carefully wrapped up all the eggs in a large plantain leaf and quickly made his way back to Dhyum.

Toshin reached back to the abandoned shrine where Dhyum was resting. The little boy who was waiting for Toshin was sent home.

Toshin looked at Dhyum and his condition was worsening, his skin was a pale blue now and there was a continuous stream of foam forming in his mouth. Doree was much better and hopping around with a limp and was by the side of his master, sniffing him and woofing at him to wake up. Doree had sniffed the smell of death around Dhyum and was greatly sorrowed and disturbed by it and when Toshin came in she woofed at him pleading with Toshin to heal his master.

'Soon Doree soon' Toshin promised her.

He sat down and tried to compose himself. He knew the next few moments were crucial for him and for Dhyum. How he handled what was to come would determine the fate of not only his dying companion but perhaps scores more in Almagri and Oleva. He closed his eyes and waited.

He smelled her before he could see her. Doree began a low growl to warn Toshin of the presence of evil as the strange smell pervaded the abandoned shrine, there seemed to be a chill in the air and silence all around as the birds and the insects suddenly fell silent.

A meditating Toshin opened his eyes and looked at the prone Dhyum, who seemed to be just as disturbed as his closed eyes were moving rapidly and he was struggling as though he was seeing a nightmare.

'Hush my friend' a nervous Toshin placed his protective hand on Dhyum's forehead and he took his place behind Dhyum, sword in hand.

She breezed in smoothly, beautiful white robes flowing all around her. Dark long hair cascading down her smooth body, tall straight and elegant. She stood in front of him holding the lizard in her arms, petting it. Smiling at him, full of joy and happiness.

Toshin gripped himself and reminded himself of the rules of engagement:

1. Never make direct eye contact with her.

2. Never let her touch you and

3. And most important never for a moment forget what she is.

Toshin looked to her left and pointed the sword at her 'Stop there' he spoke with as much authority as he could muster.

She looked at the sleeping warrior and a hint of a smile played on her lips 'You must love him dearly to take all this trouble, to risk your own life for another's. Such a noble trait', 'Look dear' she said holding up her lizard so that her lizard can have a good look at Toshin 'I thought it was a thing of the past but well, here we are facing a *man* of honour and courage.' She said "man" with scorn in her voice.

Toshin kept his eyes on them as Doree stood alert, ready to pounce on them at the first sign of trouble.

'Cure him' Toshin managed to speak.

'What? I cannot hear you' she taunted him.

'Cure him...' he said restraining himself from adding 'Please'.

'Such a fine young man, what a waste' she said 'Who do I look like to you? Do I look like a healer?' she laughed, her laugh echoing in the small chamber. 'Your love for him has made you desperate...what is your name?' she asked him.

'Never mind my name, cure him, I know you can' spoke Toshin.

'Who told you that I can heal anyone or anything?' he spoke as she casually drifted closer to the prone Dhyum.

'Just heal him' Toshin continued patiently.

'Smart boy' she laughed out loud. 'Look dear, you should learn from him' she addressed her lizard again 'Just requests, no threats, no anger. Just a sweet boy begging me to save his friends life. He is so different from all the young men who came after my family and burnt them all alive, don't you think?'

'We had nothing to do with that' Toshin countered.

'Oh yes, you and your kind did have everything to do with it, and you would do the same' she said softly but her tone was not sweet anymore.

'We were just living our life, we were not troubling anyone, we did not want anything from you and yet what did you do?' she asked softly, her voice even and smooth with no break in her rhythm 'Your famous prince rode into our forest with his army and my young brothers, sisters….all gone' she said 'You and your friend here must have all celebrated your great victory of killing my entire clan' she said.

'Look at me' she shrieked suddenly.

Toshin looked at her directly for the first time. Her face did not have the same calmness and serenity now. She had moved closer to them and was now within touching distance from Dhyum.

Doree growled slowly but made no move.

'I am sorry' said Toshin weakly.

'Sorry?' she giggled.

Toshin averted his gaze away from her again and looked at her from the corner of his eyes as tears rolled down her smooth cheeks. Toshin closed his eyes and concentrated on her smell 'Never forget what she is'

'Cure him…NOW' he screamed.

she started chuckling and it turned into a full throated laughter 'Poor weakling' she spat out with disgust 'Give me back my eggs and I will spare your miserable soul.'

'No' said a calm again Toshin. 'Cure him.'

'Silly boy' she said. Her voice was no longer the cool detached voice, it had an edge to it now 'Where are my eggs?' she spoke suddenly menacingly, her eyes were getting wider and greener and her soft skin was getting rough and scaly.

Doree stood up alert and growled at her.

Toshin raised his arm and showed her the one egg he held in his palm.

Seeing the egg the lizard started wriggled out of her hand and jumped on the floor but did not make a move 'hush dear' she quietened her agitated lizard 'Where are the rest?' she hissed 'You don't think I can find them wherever you hide them?' she hissed.

'Go ahead, what is stopping you' Toshin slowly moved the egg in front of the fire burning behind.

'Stooppp' she screamed in anger and pain 'Stooopp'

'Start now' Toshin pointed towards Dhyum 'and you will get them back otherwise you will never see them again'.

The reptile hissed at her and Toshin heard whispers in his head.

She moved towards Dhyum and studied him. 'I need time to heal him, the poison has gone deep' she said.

'Then start now' Toshin ordered 'But if you try any tricks you know what will happen.

She inspected his wounds and looked at Toshin. He heard her voice in his head, do not harm my eggs.

Toshin took a step back away from the fire but remained alert.

She removed the garments that Dhyum had worn and sniffed at the festering wounds. She started working on them by sucking out the blood and spitting it out. She then produced a glass vial and dropped a liquid in his mouth. Toshin and Doree watched in rapt attention as she continued working on Dhyum and he could already see that his skin had stopped turning blue and so had the foam that was forming in his mouth. She worked through the night sucking out the bad poisoned blood and cleaning the wounded area with the ointment the monk had sent. When it was all done she finally picked up a bowl and turned around and then turned to face Toshin with the bowl full of milk.

'He will sleep for two days now' she said 'When he wakes let him drink this'.

'Do I have your word that he is cured?' Toshin asked.

'Yes' she said 'you have my word'. She sat down exhausted from the ordeal. She was no longer the smooth skinned enchanting woman with long dark hair who had swooped in last evening, instead she was now a scaly skinned haggard looking woman with wide slanty narrow eyes and a reptilian wide slit for a mouth. She looked uncannily like the reptile she was holding.

'Swear on your eggs that he is cured.' Toshin pushed the egg towards her.

She walked up to him and extended her palm and cut herself, her blood rolled over her egg as she spoke 'I swear on my eggs.'

'Now my eggs' she said tiredly.

'One more thing' Toshin said 'Leave this forest and go far away and never return.'

She narrowed her eyes at Toshin and said 'I hate this rotten place anyway'.

He kept the egg on the sand which was quickly picked up by the reptile.

'Where are the rest of the eggs?' she demanded.

'It is in the same place I had picked it from' he said.

'And if I don't find my eggs there' the sorceress said her green eyes looking deep into Toshins, the next words were not spoken by her but Toshin heard them clearly in his head as she turned and slithered out of the chamber. *'If my eggs are harmed I will make it my mission to get rid of you and everyone you love'.*

16. Heroes Reunite

16

Heroes Reunite

They had all gathered at the farmhouse of Priyu. Priyu the gracious and grateful host was presiding over the gathering with much relish and affection. No expense was spared in making the event festive and joyous. The entire farmhouse was lit up with bright lamps of many colours and scents. Beautiful flowers and art decorated the walls and the path that led to the garden where a stage was erected. The best cooks were brought over to prepare a lavish feast of endless delicacies. There was an abundance of delicious food, fine wine, entertainment and laughter. Archika had personally supervised the preparation of the dishes and as expected had gone overboard with the number of sweet dishes made.

All the attention was of course on the two heroes Toshin and Dhyum. They gathered in the beautiful garden where they were all relaxed in comfortable cushioned Diwans's and were attended to by the servers attending to the needs of the guest. Seated together the audience listened to their exploits with rapt attention as Toshin took them through their journey through the Ajoori tribe, the adventure in the tunnel, the monk of the Austro order, the fight with the dreaded Kulgi and ultimately the faceoff with the sorceress. He enjoyed his role as he explained with much gusto to the awe and appreciation of the audience.

Apart from Priyu and his wife there was the Chariot woman Sanigya was with two of her assistants, Fauja was more interested in the fine wine and made his appreciation abundant and his cup was filled regularly. The artifact merchant of Oleva was also present and by special invitation from Priyu, Doree took his place proudly next to his master Dhyum and nuzzled upto Dhyum at regular intervals.

There was much toasting as Priyu, Fauja and Sanigya got up to congratulate the heroes and thank them for their valour and selflessness in safeguarding the citizens of the Almagri Kingdom.

Sanigya slided upto Dhyum and gave her warm blessings. She looked at Dhyum and inspected his healing wounds 'I am glad to see that you are getting well soon' she blessed Dhyum. 'And where's the naughty one?' she asked turning to find Toshin regaling her two young beautiful assistants with their exploits. 'I will spare him today' she smiled mischievously at Dhyum. 'I wanted to know something, Can we trust the word of a sorceress?' she asked Dhyum.

'I believe she has more to lose than us' said Dhyum. 'After we started hunting and terminating all creatures of their kind, they were left with few places to hide and even fewer of their kind. I suspect that the eggs were precious to her as they were the last hope for the survival of their kind'.

The chariot woman was thoughtful 'hmm sometimes I wonder who are the heroes and who are the villians here' she said.

'So you expect that Oleva will not attack us now?' she asked him.

'He was banking on the magic potion of this woman to galvanise the lost morale of his troops, he will make another attempt and we have to be prepared for that again' he said.

Their conversation was interrupted by the garrulous Fauja, he called out loudly to Priyu 'Priyu, where is the surprise you had announced'.

'All in good time Fauja' Priyu said good naturedly 'I hope you are enjoying the food as well?'

'Of course, what do you mean?' Fauja sat up spilling a little of the wine.

'Archika will be very upset if you do not do the feast justice' Priyu warned him.

The merchant spoke up raising his cup 'Honorable Priyu, I am extremely grateful that you have included me and my family in this feast which is fit for a King'.

'My dear friend, we cannot thank you enough for your services to the Kingdom, how could we not include you' said Priyu and quickly added as something caught his attention 'and you what you mentioned is right, this feast is fit for a King' and so saying he turned around welcoming the King of Almagri as the King Smrikruta of Almagri made his grand entrance with his troop.

They all rose up stunned and surprised by the arrival of the King of Almargi in all his glory walking with his queen besides him in all her splendor and elegance. Prince Brihu walked closely behind and Priyu was relieved to see that the Prince walked with only a trace of the limp. The prince Brihu was wearing the special limb made for him by the Chariot lady Sanigya. Xyree walked proudly behind the queen followed by maids and servants carrying gifts and presents.

They all bowed down and saluted the King. The King, Queen and Prince Brihu were greeted by Priyu who guided them to their seat of honour but before taking their seats they walked over to the bowing Toshin and Dhyum.

'Please everyone sit down' the King addressed them 'This is a joyous occasion and a moment of great joy, maybe we can disregard some of the formalities today? What do you say Priyu?' he looked towards Priyu smiling as the rest of the gathered guests also smiled their approval. Even the stoic Priyu threw his hands up in the air happily accepting the Kings proposal.

The King turned towards the heroes of the day and spoke to them 'On behalf of the people of Almagri and our royal family we thank you and salute you for your brave deeds. The soil of Almagri is indeed very fortunate to have sons and daughters like you all present here which makes this Kingdom what it is today. We will be ever indebted.'

'Glory to Almagri and Glory to the Sun god' he called out and was joined by all the guests raising their cups.

'Now Priyu' he turned towards him 'I cannot wait for the surprise you have arranged for us' he said.

Priyu ushered the King and queen to their seats and clapped his hands. The sweet strains of the veena filled air as the curtain was raised from the stage.

There sat Priyu's wife with her Veena. Even the King sat up straight as they all gasped in surprise at the sight of Priyu's wife with the Veena. She who had not performed for years and years and had deprived the people of Almagri the soul capturing magic of her Veena was once again playing the beautiful instrument as a proud Priyu beamed on.

The music rose up in the night sky as it bound them in its magical spell.

About the Author

Based in Dubai, Omi is of Indian origin. His outlook and ideals have been shaped by his experiences and travels throughout Asia and Africa. He draws inspiration from his interactions and immersion in different cultures and belief systems.

When not writing columns or stories, he prefers spending time on the tennis court, climbing mountains or building music systems.